He didn't want Julie hanging out with any of her friends. That blue-eyed guy, for example, who kept looking at Julie, touching her, trying to make her laugh . . . it had taken all his self-control not to go over there and knock that guy around.

But that guy wasn't worth losing his cool over. Julie didn't even like him, Quinn could tell.

He chuckled. Julie was a prize worth winning. And when she was his, they would be together, and happy, forever. Just the two of them. They wouldn't need anyone else.

She would make him forget the terrible parts of his life. His father. Alison. The Place.

But what if her friends tried to interfere, like last time, the way Alison's had?

Let them try. They'd be sorry if they did. He was older and smarter now. He knew how to handle creeps like that.

Yes, he'd make them sorry if they did.

And this time he wouldn't get caught.

Read these terrifying thrillers
from HarperPaperbacks!

Baby-sitter's Nightmare
Sweet Dreams
Sweetheart
Teen Idol
Running Scared
by Kate Daniel

And look for:

Class Trip
by Bebe Faas Rice

The Nightmare Inn series
#1 *Nightmare Inn*
#2 *Room 13*
#3 *The Pool*
#4 *The Attic*
by T. S. Rue

LOVE YOU TO DEATH

BEBE FAAS RICE

HarperPaperbacks

A Division of HarperCollins*Publishers*

HarperPaperbacks *A Division of* HarperCollins*Publishers*
10 East 53rd Street, New York, N.Y. 10022

Copyright © 1994 by Bebe Faas Rice and
Daniel Weiss Associates, Inc.

Cover art copyright © 1994 Daniel Weiss Associates, Inc.

Produced by Daniel Weiss Associates, Inc., 33 West 17th Street,
New York, New York 10011.

First printing: May 1994

Printed in the United States of America

HarperPaperbacks and colophon are trademarks of
HarperCollins*Publishers*

10 9 8 7 6 5 4 3 2 1

To Marie and John, with love.

CHAPTER ONE

Afterward—for the rest of her life, in fact—Julie Hagan would wonder at the suddenness of it.

One moment was all it took. One brief moment and her life was changed forever.

"Wow, check that out!" Shelley Molino said, her Bambi-brown eyes widening, as she stared over Julie's shoulder toward the entrance to the cafeteria.

Julie set her loaded tray on the table, the special table reserved by unspoken law for members of Jefferson High's elite "in" group.

Then she turned and followed Shelley's gaze.

And caught her breath as the boy in the doorway looked back at her.

Even at this distance, halfway across the

1

busy, noisy school cafeteria, Julie-felt drawn to him. Felt the sudden, almost physical current that seemed to flow between them. Deep inside her, she felt everything—heart, stomach, whatever—give an odd little lurch. She pressed her hand to her mouth, almost frightened by her reaction to him.

What's happening to me? she thought. *And why? Is it his looks? Or is it the way he's staring at me?*

The boy had stepped to the side of the entrance now, away from the crowd of students that surged through the door behind him. He was leaning against the wall, his hands in the pockets of his faded jeans, a slight frown on his face. And he was staring at her.

Yes, staring. She was sure it was at her.

His eyes . . . so dark, so intense. Were they black? Blue-black, maybe? It was hard to tell from here.

He isn't exactly what you'd call handsome, Julie thought, trying to collect her wits. *Rugged? Yeah. Sexy? Definitely sexy, and there's something about the way he's standing that tells you he knows how to take care of himself.*

"Hey, Tara," Jessica Claggett said, her voice breaking through Julie's daze. "Has that guy over there got a thing for you, or what?"

Tara, Julie thought, dismayed. *He's been staring at Tara, not me!*

Julie hoped she didn't look as humiliated as she felt. What on earth made her think *she* was the one he'd been watching so intently? He probably hadn't even noticed her standing there, gawking at him with her mouth hanging open. At least she hoped he hadn't. She must have looked like a total jerk!

He had been staring at Tara Braxton, the resident Southern belle. Her ancestors had founded this small but classy little town and then modestly named it after themselves: Braxton Falls, Virginia. Braxton Falls on the Potomac. Tara's social credentials in this part of the country carried a lot of weight.

Yes, he was watching Tara, all right. Naturally. Who else rated that kind of attention? Tara and Jessica had come to the table right after Julie. They'd been standing behind her the whole time. And *he'd* been looking past her at Tara, while she'd mistakenly thought that . . .

And yet . . .

No. It was always Tara who got the cute ones. Gorgeous Tara with her thick, straight black hair and long-lashed gray eyes. She was the one boys looked at first.

Julie sat down at the table, taking care to turn her back on *him*. She'd show him she'd known all along just who it was he'd been staring at. And that she didn't care.

Tara sat down facing her and preened a little, stealing a quick glance across the room from under lowered lashes.

"Has *who* got a thing for me, Jess? If you mean that gorgeous six-foot hunk over by the door, I haven't noticed."

Jessica and Shelley laughed appreciatively. They had been friends with Tara since grade school, but they still acted a little too eager to please. They were constantly flattering Tara, trying desperately to keep on her good side.

"You were saying yesterday you hoped we'd get some new guys at school this year," Shelley said to Tara. "Well, this one is definitely new. We'd all remember *him* if he'd ever set foot in this place before."

"Shelley, don't keep looking at him!" Tara scolded. "I don't want him to know we're talking about him. I'm going to play hard to get with this one." She laughed and a dimple flashed briefly in one cheek. "This will definitely make things more interesting around here. He's mine, starting right now, so hands off, everybody."

4

"If you've set your sights on him, Tara, the poor guy doesn't stand a chance," Jessica said, smiling.

Tara flipped back her long hair and looked pleased.

She really likes this, Julie thought. *She likes having this power over people. That's what her looks and money and social status mean to her. Power over the rest of us.*

Julie wondered why she hung out with Tara and the others. She'd been wondering that a lot recently. Why, when she certainly knew better, had she tied herself up with this snobby little trio who didn't believe in associating with what they called "losers and dweebs"? Anyone outside their small circle of carefully selected class beauties, student-body leaders, and top-notch school athletes was considered beneath their notice.

Julie sighed, picked up her fork, and poked at her food. Mystery meat again, covered with some kind of runny-looking sauce.

"Don't look now—Shelley, don't turn around!—but Mr. Sexpot is going through the cafeteria line," Jessica reported in a stage whisper. "Maybe he'll come this way. Wait . . . no . . . he's going to the corner where the science nerds hang out—that ought to give creepy Norine Goldsmith the thrill of her life."

"I don't think Norine's all that interested in boys right now," Julie said.

"Why not?" Jessica asked. "'Cause she likes computers better?"

"No. Norine's trying to get a scholarship to Cal Tech, and that's the most important thing in her life right now. I wouldn't expect you to understand that, Jessica."

Julie hadn't meant to sound so cold and hostile. It had simply come out that way, and it was too late to change it now. Fortunately, it was hard to insult Jessica. Things seemed to bounce right off her.

"Well, pardon me, Miss Priss," Jessica responded, making a face. "Aren't we touchy today, defending the nerds and making life safe for democracy?"

"Girls! Girls!" said Tara. "All for one and one for all, remember? We're friends, okay?"

Julie suddenly felt tired. Tired and bored.

What's wrong with me? she wondered. *Must just be the back-to-school blues.*

She glanced off to the far corner, to the science nerds' table. *He* looked as good from the back as he did from the front.

Am I jealous of Tara? Is that it?

No. It wasn't just that. Julie wasn't surprised by Tara's going after the new guy. But she'd been feeling critical of Tara, Jessica, and Shelley for several months now. Before last summer, even. She'd been friends with them ever since she moved to Braxton Falls three years ago. She'd been a shy eighth-grader then, eager for acceptance. She'd been thrilled when the three prettiest, most popular girls in her class included her in their group.

"Three's a bad number," Tara had explained. "You know—two's company and three's a crowd and all that. Somebody always feels left out when there are only three of you. Four is much, much better."

But now that she was sixteen and a junior at Jefferson High, Julie didn't like being a member of Tara's foursome anymore. They acted so silly and shallow sometimes. But still, hanging out with them did mean she was always included in the band of popular kids that revolved around Tara.

And if she *did* stop hanging out with Tara and the others, her last two years at Jefferson High might be pretty miserable. Tara would probably see to it that she was snubbed as a punishment for her disloyalty. She'd done it before to a girl who'd made her mad, and Julie didn't think she was strong enough to cope with treatment like that.

And besides, she thought with a shrug, *why should I do something crazy like that, anyway? Who wouldn't want to be one of the movers and shakers of Jefferson High? They're the ones who make things happen and have all the fun. And it makes Mom happy that I'm friends with Tara.*

For Julie's mother, moving to prestigious Braxton Falls had been the realization of all her girlhood dreams.

When her husband parlayed a small restaurant into a modest chain of fast-food diners, Mrs. Hagan talked him into moving to Braxton Falls and buying a huge custom-built home in Hunter Valley, an area that had once belonged to Tara's aristocratic ancestors. And nothing thrilled her more than knowing that her daughter was considered good enough to be friends with one of the famous Braxtons.

The cafeteria table was filling up now, and Julie found herself squashed between Brad Stafford, junior-class playboy, and Nick Wells, the editor of the school paper.

"You're awfully quiet today, gorgeous," Brad

said, flashing his famous, even-toothed smile, the smile that could bring every girl at Jefferson High to her knees.

Well, almost every girl. Julie was the exception. Brad wasn't her type. For one thing, he was too good-looking, with that blond hair, and those blue eyes and white teeth. She didn't trust all that perfection. He was always pretending to come on to her lately, hamming it up as he grabbed her knee or played footsie with her. Julie found it all really embarrassing.

At this very minute she could feel his thigh jammed up against hers, from hip to knee. Of course, the table was crowded, but he was sitting a little closer than he had to. And when he started wriggling his eyebrows at her, Julie decided she'd had enough.

Furious, she planted an elbow in his side and shoved. Hard.

"Ouch!" he gasped, moving away from her. "Geez, Julie, take it easy, will you? Can't a guy get a little friendly around here without you laying on the ninja stuff?"

"Go get friendly with someone else, Romeo," she snapped.

"You're beautiful when you're angry," Brad said, rubbing his side gingerly.

Tara waved him to silence with a fluttering motion of her hand and leaned forward across the table, lowering her voice.

"Listen, guys, does anybody know anything about that new boy? The tall, good-looking one?"

This is her way of playing hard to get? Julie thought, amused. *By the time school lets out today, everyone within earshot will know that Tara Braxton's going after the new guy.*

"He's a senior, that's all I know," Nick Wells offered. "And he's from out of town. I don't know why he's a couple weeks late starting school, though."

"Isn't he great?" asked Lisa Doyle, sighing. "What a hunk!"

Lisa was one of the best cheerleaders at Jefferson High. A slim, compact little blonde, she combined top-quality gymnastics with her routines.

"I was over by the principal's office when he checked in this morning," she went on. "Naturally, I asked around about him, but all anyone knows is that his name's Quinn McNeal, and that he's eighteen and a senior. Karen Slack works part-time in the office. She promised to find out everything she can about him."

"There are a couple of rumors going around about him," said Colin King. As the captain of the football team, Colin had probably looked the newcomer over with an eye toward recruiting him, Julie figured. Quinn was certainly big enough.

"I don't know where they started," Colin said. "One kid told me he's a former dropout from another town who's come back to school to finish his education. But then someone else said he was orphaned in some kind of accident and that he's been in the hospital for a long time because of it."

"That explains why he looks older than other senior guys," Lisa said. "And Karen heard him tell the principal's secretary he lives alone in a basement apartment in town, so the orphan rumor must be true."

"Hmmm," Tara said, her eyes glowing. "He gets more interesting by the minute. He's a real mystery man, isn't he?"

When they got up to leave the cafeteria, Julie took a quick look around, hoping to get another glimpse of Quinn. She had to see if he would affect her the same way this time as he had before.

He wasn't there.

A terrible feeling of loneliness swept over Julie. She felt abandoned.

And then she saw him. It was almost as if he'd been waiting for her.

He was standing in a dark corner of the hall. And he was looking at *her*—she was sure of it—not at Tara.

Julie tried not to stare at him.

His hair was dark and thick, with an unruly lock that fell over his forehead. His cheekbones were prominent in his lean face, and his nose looked as if it had been broken at some time in the past—it was a little flattened across the bridge. Julie thought it only made his face more interesting, more masculine.

And his mouth, with that full, finely sculpted upper lip . . .

Julie turned away, her heart beating erratically, and took a deep breath. She wondered what it would be like to kiss that mouth.

CHAPTER TWO

I can't believe it, he thought. *That girl, that beautiful girl, with the crowd of giggling, silly cheerleader types . . .*

For a minute I thought she was Alison. Same long golden-brown hair. Same big amber-colored eyes. I could see their color, even from where I stood.

And the way she looked at me—almost as if she recognized me. I could swear she recognized me.

But she wasn't Alison. How could she be? Alison is . . . gone.

And then later, in the hall, when she'd drawn a breath and turned away. That faint flush on her cheeks, and the way her pulse fluttered in her throat. He'd seen it fluttering like a butterfly in the hollow of that beautiful, creamy-skinned little throat. Her skin was like silk. He could imagine the feel and scent of that warm, living silk. . . .

No, he cautioned himself. *I mustn't think of that now. Not yet. I rushed it last time . . . and look what happened. This time I'll take it slow and easy. I'll make her wonder, make her want me to make my move. But first she has to notice me, and I think she has.*

He smiled. A thin, faint scar, running downward, bisected his upper lip, giving him a slightly crooked, arrogant-looking smile. Like a pirate, someone had told him once.

Yes, she noticed me all right, he thought. *And I could tell she felt the same thing for me that I feel for her. She knows me. She's always known me, just as I've always known her.*

He liked slender girls, he liked the look of slender frailty, and she was as slim and willowy as a princess, just as Alison had been. And she had that same proud, graceful way of moving her pretty little body.

He frowned.

But she's not Alison, he told himself. *I've got to stop thinking of Alison and looking for her in every face I see. That part of my life is over. And didn't I pay a high enough price for it? Four years in*

The Place, and the terrible loneliness of knowing I must live a lifetime without Alison.

And yet . . . that girl. That girl with the amber-brown eyes.

Am I being given a second chance?

CHAPTER THREE

The big news at school the next day was that there was no news.

"Quinn McNeal's records aren't with any of the others," Karen Slack told Lisa Doyle, who promptly passed it along.

Julie, Tara, Shelley, and Jessica were at their lockers before third period when Lisa excitedly gave them the news.

". . . And Karen says she's sure Mr. Reed's got them locked up in his special file," Lisa concluded. "But why do you think he'd do something like that?"

Tara closed her locker carefully and shifted her books from one arm to the other. Her gray eyes narrowed.

"My, my," she murmured. "This Quinn McNeal

16

gets more mysterious all the time, doesn't he?"

"Maybe he's really some exiled prince or something, and we're not supposed to find out!" Shelley said breathlessly.

"That is so dumb, Shelley," Jessica said. "Why would he come down here? He could go to a fancy prep school up north, if he was so rich."

"Well, if he isn't a prince, he should be," Shelley insisted. "He looks like one, doesn't he, Julie?"

"He's . . . he's very . . . good-looking," Julie agreed. She felt a blush begin at the collar of her blouse and work its way upward, toward her hairline. Oh, why couldn't she grow out of this stupid, babyish habit she had of blushing?

Julie saw Tara eye her closely. Her scarlet lips were set in a thin line.

"Just to set the record straight," Tara said evenly, tapping a long fingernail on her notebook, "you all *did* hear me when I said that Quinn McNeal is on my list of things to do, didn't you? I'd hate to see somebody get in the way."

She made her point well. *She always does,* Julie thought rebelliously. *And what would she do, I wonder, if somebody actually dared to disobey her?*

*　　*　　*

17

Wild speculations about Quinn and his missing school records continued at lunchtime. But Julie wasn't paying attention to her friends. Without even looking up from her plate, she could feel Quinn's eyes on her.

Am I imagining this? Julie wondered. She knew she could look over and see for herself if he was watching. But somehow she couldn't make her eyes turn toward Quinn. *Anyway, if he is looking,* she thought, *what am I supposed to do about it?*

Quinn was at the far end of the cafeteria again, not at the table with the science nerds—at another one, even farther away. But this time he was facing Julie.

Or Tara.

It was obvious that Tara thought he was looking at her, Tara Braxton, the hottest thing in the South since Scarlett O'Hara. She was doing her animated, pink-cheeked, sparkling-eyed thing, the way she always did when she was out to let some guy know she was available.

Julie noticed how Tara made a point of not looking over at Quinn, while still managing to make it clear she was playing to him, teasing him into noticing her.

Nick Wells, sitting beside Tara, looked upset.

Julie saw the angry pulse that beat in his temple. His fingers tightened on the edge of his tray, knuckles whitening suddenly when Tara flung back her long hair and laughed her special there's-a-boy-watching laugh.

Nick was no fool. Julie had always respected his intelligence. It was obvious he knew what Tara was up to—hadn't she come onto him the same way last June when he'd been named editor of the school paper?

Tara only went for the important guys, the rich ones or the ones who wielded some kind of power on campus. Nick was well aware of that. He knew Tara was using him. He'd admitted it to Julie, who worked on the staff of the school newspaper with him.

"It doesn't matter, Julie," he'd said. "I'll take Tara on any terms. I'm crazy about her—always have been. But this is the first time I've ever gotten anywhere with her."

He and Tara had been a hot item all summer, and Nick obviously had been counting on it to continue.

And now Tara was making a play for the new guy.

"Anyway, Karen says there's no way she can get access to Quinn's records if—" Lisa was saying.

19

Nick cut in on her. "Isn't it about time we went on to some other subject around here? I'm sick of hearing about Quinn McNeal."

Lisa sniffed. "Just because we're *mildly* interested in the administrative handling of our records here at Jefferson High . . ."

"You're all trying to snoop into this guy McNeal's private business, that's what you're doing. And there's probably nothing mysterious about him at all," Nick said. "We all know that Mr. Reed's too old and absentminded to be a principal. I'll bet he lost those records and doesn't want to admit it."

"Nick's right," Brad agreed. "That poor old guy can't even find his own rear end with both hands."

"What a disgusting thing to say," Tara said.

Brad put on an injured, innocent expression, blue eyes opened wide. "I was only trying to be helpful"

Tara looked sideways at Nick, arching one perfectly plucked eyebrow, and smiled playfully.

She's being cute now, trying to charm Nick, Julie thought disgustedly. *Just in case things don't work out with the new guy.*

Tara's lips were soft and pouty as she leaned toward Nick. "I know somebody who got out of bed on the wrong side this morning—"

"You mean you were there, you wild thing?" Brad asked with an exaggerated leer. "Does your mother know?"

Tara ignored him. "—and I think I'd better see if I can do something to sweeten him up."

She leaned over and kissed Nick on the tip of his nose.

A soft, dopey look immediately came over his face. *Like Silly Putty*, Julie thought. *I wish I knew how she does it.*

"Hey, Julie, how about sweetening *me* up? I'm feeling mean as a snake today," Brad said, reaching under the table and groping for her knee.

"No wonder. You *are* a snake!" Julie retorted, getting to her feet and gathering up her trash.

From the corner of her eye, she could see Quinn rise from his seat and head her way. No, not her way exactly. Toward the trash bin. The same one she was heading for. They were going to arrive there at exactly the same moment!

He's been waiting for me, Julie thought with dead certainty. *Watching me and waiting for me to get up so he can make his move. He's planned this "accidental" meeting so that he can . . .*

So that he could what? Talk to her? Introduce himself?

Or meet Tara?

But Julie knew that it definitely wasn't Tara. It was Julie.

But why?

I'm no competition for Tara, she thought. *I'm pretty enough, but Tara's a stunner. A guy like that deserves a stunner.*

And yet Julie had known all along that something was happening between Quinn McNeal and herself. It had started yesterday. That was the first step, today was the second.

Julie stood before the garbage bin, not looking up. She could see long legs in faded jeans beside hers. There was the beginning of a small, ragged hole in the knee of one pant leg.

Quinn reached out and took her tray, his hand brushing hers in passing.

A shock went through Julie. Startled, she looked up and met his gaze.

He felt it, too, she thought. *There's no way he couldn't have noticed that connection.*

Julie's cheeks felt warm. Her neck. Her ears. She was suddenly very aware of every cell in her body.

They stood looking at each other for what seemed an eternity. She realized later that it had only been several seconds. But in those seconds the noise of the room seemed to dim and she was aware of only him. The way he stood. That faint scar on his lip.

And then he smiled, just the beginning of a smile. Before Julie could respond, before she could snap out of her reverie, he upended her tray with one quick flick of the wrist, sending her uneaten pizza and milk carton into the bin. Then he laid the tray on the conveyor belt that trundled it off to the kitchen.

Julie realized her hand was outstretched, as if she were still holding her tray. Blushing, she dropped it to her side. He gave her another quick little sketch of a smile, turned on his heel, and was gone.

I still don't know what color his eyes are, Julie thought dazedly. *Black, or dark blue?*

"My, my, isn't our new student helpful?" said a voice in her ear. Tara wasn't cooing now. Her voice was rock-hard and edged with steel.

Julie turned and faced her.

Tara's eyes were a flat slate-gray and cold as a winter sky.

"It was *me* he wanted to meet, Julie, but you had to rush right over and make a fool of yourself, didn't you? Next time, butt out!"

Chapter Four

Julie waited until later, when Tara had cooled down, before attempting to talk to her.

"Look, Tara, about what happened between Quinn and me—"

"What *did* happen between you and Quinn, Julie?"

"Well, nothing, but—"

"Right. And that's why I got so upset." Tara opened her eyes wide, trying to look sincere and caring. "It was really pathetic. If only you could have seen the way you stared at him! Honestly, Julie, I was *so* embarrassed for you. I mean, I'm one of your very best friends, and it really hurt me to see you acting like such a dweeb."

"I didn't stare at him," Julie lied.

"Trust me, Julie. You were definitely *not*

cool." Tara threw an arm around Julie. "Look, I'm the one Quinn's coming on to, so don't make a fool of yourself over him, okay?"

With another fake smile, Tara turned her back and sauntered off down the hall. Julie sighed and headed into her classroom. She sat next to Jessica in biology. Usually, before class started, they'd talk and laugh together. Today it was different. Jessica opened her notebook and began to look through her notes from the previous day, studiously ignoring Julie.

Julie laid her hand on Jessica's arm. "Aren't you speaking to me today, Jess?"

Jessica raised her head in pretended surprise. "Oh, sure, Julie. What's up?"

I'm in love, that's what's up, Julie longed to say. *Talk to me about love at first sight, Jess. Does it really happen? Does it last? And what should I do about it?*

Instead she said, "Tara's really mad at me, isn't she?"

Jessica looked away. "Well, it really wasn't fair of you to make a move on Quinn McNeal, Julie. After all, Tara said she liked him, didn't she?"

"But I didn't make a move on him," Julie protested feebly.

"Tara says you did," Jessica said flatly.

And whatever Tara says, you believe. Aren't you my friend, too, Jess? Everybody thinks you are. They envy the four of us, they think we're the best of friends—close enough to tell each other everything.

"So you think I tried to beat Tara out, is that it?" Julie asked.

Jessica shifted in her chair. "Let's just say, Julie, that the four of us have to be loyal to each other. I mean, we've been together for a long time. And Tara's always been a good friend to you and Shelley and me, hasn't she?"

Maybe we've never really been friends, the four of us, Julie thought. *Maybe we've only been using each other all these years.*

"Sort of," she answered Jessica.

"Sort of?" Jessica's eyes, normally placid, shot off sparks. "What do you mean, *sort of?* Where would you be now if Tara hadn't taken you under her wing when you came to Braxton Falls three years ago? You were a nobody then, Julie!"

Maybe I'd be with the science nerds, Julie thought dreamily. *Or the literary crowd. And I might feel more comfortable and happier around them than I do around you and Tara.*

26

"So where would you be?" Jessica repeated angrily.

"Nowhere, I guess," Julie replied wearily, opening her biology book. "Nowhere at all."

For the first time in her life, Julie was in love. And with a boy she hadn't even spoken to yet. She longed to talk to somebody about him. To say his name aloud to a sympathetic ear: QuinnQuinnQuinnQuinnQuinn!

But who could she talk to about it?

Not Jess or Shelley, that was clear, now. Lisa Doyle, maybe? No, not her. Lisa would have it all over school by first period tomorrow.

Her mother? *Forget it!* Julie thought. *If Mom knew the kind of feelings I have for Quinn, she'd give me that outdated lecture about the birds and the bees again. Of course, there's always Mollie. . . .*

That night, after supper, Julie rapped on her sister's bedroom door.

"Come in!"

Julie smiled to herself as she turned the doorknob. How many girls her age would turn to a fourteen-year-old sister for advice? But Mollie was different. She was funny, incredibly intelligent, and could always be trusted to keep a secret.

Mollie was curled up on her bed, reading glasses perched on the end of her nose, a thick novel propped on her knees.

"Would you believe *War and Peace?*" she asked, making a face. "Ms. Landsburg is giving extra credit to anyone who finished it this semester. It's really not bad, though, once you get used to all those complicated Russian names."

Mollie's room looked more like an office than a teenage girl's bedroom. No ruffles and stuffed animals for her. Everything was spartan, pared down, intellectual looking. "Early bookworm," their mother called it.

Bur Mollie wasn't really a bookworm. Her "thing" was computers. She wasn't just a computer nut, she was a computer genius. So were her friends, especially her best friend, Tommy Tomagawa. Julie envied the fun they seemed to have together, their lack of pretense, and the way they talked to each other from the heart.

Julie sank down in the wing chair by the bed. "Look, Mollie, I need to talk."

Mollie immediately closed her book and took off her glasses. "Sure. Shoot."

"It's about this guy, Mollie. I need your advice."

Mollie hooted with laughter. "You've got to

be kidding! Me? Give you advice on your love life?"

She stopped laughing when she noticed her sister's serious expression.

"But you're the social wheeler and dealer in the family, Julie," she protested. "I thought *you* had all the answers. What on earth do I know about guys and dating?"

"Not much, I admit," Julie said. "But you're the only one I can talk to about it right now. You've got to keep it quiet, though. Just between the two of us, okay?"

"If you say so." Mollie drew a cross over her heart. "Hope to die."

"There's this guy—" Julie began.

"What's his name?"

"I don't think you know him. He's a new senior. His name's Quinn McNeal."

Mollie sat bolt upright. Her book slipped off her knees and to the floor.

"Quinn McNeal? *That* one? Are we really talking about *the* Quinn McNeal?"

"What do you know about him?"

"Only that as of nine A.M. yesterday, every freshman girl got a case of the mad hots for him, that's what I know about Quinn McNeal. Everyone but me, of course, because I happen to

29

be incredibly cool and laid-back for my age. So what about him?"

"I know you're probably not going to believe this, Mollie, but I think Quinn's interested in me."

"You? Wow!"

Mollie put her head to one side and squinted at Julie thoughtfully. Then she nodded.

"Okay. I believe it. Why not? You're pretty. You could get just about any boy you wanted. Lots of guys like you. They always have."

Julie was touched by her little sister's praise. Mollie wasn't one to pass out empty compliments.

"It isn't just a question of like," she said. "It's a little more than that. . . . I mean, I *think* it's more than that. I hope so anyway, because I . . ."

"Julie, what are you talking about? What's happened here? The guy just checked in yesterday. What goes on in the junior-senior locker area, anyway?"

"I wish I knew what's going on," Julie said. "Please don't laugh, but I feel like someone in a movie or a book. I took one look at him yesterday and—I swear, Mollie—it happened. All those things you read about. It was like . . . like electricity . . . and . . ."

30

She stopped and looked down, blushing. "And now I can't get him out of my mind. It's like I'm obsessed with him or something."

Mollie thoughtfully chewed on a thumbnail, a habit she'd been trying to break.

"A *coup de foudre*," she said, almost reverently.

"A what?"

Mollie cleared her throat and repeated it. "It's what the French call a *coup de foudre*. A lightning bolt. Love. Freely translated, it means love's just knocked your socks off." Mollie thought for a minute. "But what about him? Are you sure he feels that same way?"

Julie nodded. "I think so. It's the way he looks at me, Mollie. He just stares at me. I can't even describe what it's like, and how it makes me feel. And today . . . he kept watching me and watching me all through lunch. I didn't even have to turn around and look. I could *feel* him looking at me. And then when I got up to dump my tray, he was there. He took my tray and his hand touched mine, and I felt it again. That electricity thing."

"Your magnetic force field," Mollie said. "We all have them surrounding us. The Russians or somebody invented a camera that can actually photograph it and—"

"Mollie! Can you give your scientific expertise a rest for a minute and talk about me?"

"Oh, sorry. So when this electric thing happened between you, what did he say?"

"Nothing. That's the strange thing. He didn't say anything. Just smiled a little and walked away. And I didn't say anything, either. It was like I was struck dumb or something."

Mollie snorted. "That's a first."

"Am I being silly? Can something like this *really* happen so fast? I only saw him for the first time yesterday, and we haven't even spoken to each other yet."

"*Romeo and Juliet* took place in only four days," Mollie said dreamily. "Four days from the eyes-across-the-room bit to the double suicide in the tomb."

"*This* is your way of cheering me up?"

"Well, Romeo and Juliet were a year or so younger than you, Julie, and obviously a little more impulsive."

"So what should I do . . . and why am I asking you about this, anyway?" Julie said.

"Because you're desperate," Mollie said with an unconcerned grin. "And because you want me to tell you to do exactly what you've been planning to do all along. So, okay, I'll say it."

She leaned forward, like a judge over a courtroom desk. "Go for it, Julie, go for it. Follow your instincts."

"You mean it?"

"Yup. These things happen, so why worry because it seems a little unusual? Or because it isn't happening to any of your airhead friends?"

"Oh!" Julie put her hand to her mouth, remembering Tara. "That's the other problem, Mollie. Tara wants Quinn for herself. She really got on my case this afternoon about him."

"So what? She can't always be the belle of the ball."

"Yeah, but she really got mean about it. She could make my life miserable."

"I could never figure out why you're friends with her in the first place," Mollie said. "What kind of friend acts that way?"

"She's not that bad, really," Julie protested halfheartedly.

"Oh, yeah?"

"I mean, we've been friends since—"

Mollie rolled her eyes. "I know. You were a shy little eighth-grade nothing until Tara made you a star. And the old 'we've been friends for years' bit."

"Well, she did, Mollie. And we have been

friends for years. Doesn't that mean anything?"

"It might mean, sister dear, that it's high time you moved on to more enriching, fulfilling friendships. There are lots of interesting kids at Jefferson High—and most of them won't boss you around all the time the way old Bubblehead does."

"Boy, Mollie," Julie said, laughing in spite of herself. "When somebody asks you for advice, you really give it."

"I give full value for your nickel," Mollie said. Then she added, "But I wouldn't worry, Julie. If Quinn goes for you, not Tara, she won't want to lose face. She'll probably try to act as if nothing's wrong, don't you think?"

"Maybe. And maybe it's time I stopped trying to please Tara. I'm not a lonely little eighth-grader anymore."

"That's more like it!"

Julie got up from the wing chair, bent over her sister, and kissed the top of her head.

"Thanks, Mollie."

"For what?"

"For everything. For being here. And for listening. I just needed someone to talk to, I guess."

CHAPTER FIVE

She was beautiful, even more beautiful up close than he'd realized.

More beautiful than Alison? Yes, in a softer, sweeter, more vulnerable way.

There'd been something a little hard and uncaring about Alison. Those girls she'd hung out with had done it to her. It should have been *them*, not Alison . . .

No, he wasn't going to think about that anymore. Not now, when he had Julie to love.

Julie. He savored the taste of her name on his lips. Julie.

My Julie.

He stretched out on his narrow bed and put his hands beneath his head, seeing her face—Julie's face—on his ceiling, replaying every delicious, exciting moment of their meeting today.

Those eyes. That hair. The way she'd looked at him when he'd taken her tray and their fingers touched.

She'd felt it, too, he could tell. That sudden, warm little shock when flesh brushed against flesh.

She'd blushed. He loved the way it had tinted her face so delicately, calling attention to the fine bones of her cheeks and forehead.

I wonder what she's doing now, he thought. *Is she thinking of me?*

Yes, of course. She has to be. If I'm thinking of her, she's thinking of me. It's almost as if there's an invisible cord connecting us. She tugs and I feel the pull. I tug, and she feels it.

He'd tested that today, in the cafeteria. He'd looked at her, willing her to feel his eyes on her. And she had. He could tell. She wanted to turn around and look at him.

He smiled fondly.

She probably didn't think he noticed her looking at him out of the corner of her eyes. Well, she'd learn very soon that he was aware of everything she did. Every breath she took.

Soon. But not right away. He'd wait just a little longer. Build up the suspense, the anticipation, both for himself and for her. You always appreciated something more when you've had to think about it, hope for it, yearn for it.

He was sure she wouldn't spoil it by coming up and talking to him. She wasn't like that. She wasn't one of those loud, bold girls.

Her friend, now, that black-haired one with the blood-red lipstick, had done her best to make him notice her.

He frowned and uttered an expression of disgust, remembering the way she'd kept throwing her body around like an alley cat and laughing in that stupid, empty-headed way.

And *she* was Julie's friend? His Julie?

No, she wasn't right for Julie. Julie was perfect, but that friend of hers was a bad apple. A corrupter. Not fit to be around the girl he loved.

In fact, he didn't want Julie hanging out with any of them. That blue-eyed guy, for example, who kept looking at Julie, touching her, trying to make her laugh . . . It had taken all his willpower and self-control not to go over there and knock that guy flat on his rich, pampered little butt.

But that blue-eyed guy wasn't worth losing his cool over. Julie didn't even like him. Quinn could tell by the way she looked at him, her lips pressed together primly with disapproval.

He chuckled. She was a prize worth winning, all right. And when he did win her, they would be together, and happy, forever.

Just the two of them. They wouldn't need anyone else.

She would make him forget the terrible parts of his life. His father. Alison. The Place.

He rolled over and adjusted the pillow under his head.

But what if her friends tried to interfere, like last time, the way Alison's had?

Let them try. They'd be sorry if they did. He was older and smarter now. He knew how to handle creeps like that.

Yes, he'd make them sorry if they did.

And this time he wouldn't get caught.

CHAPTER SIX

"Hey, Julie! Wait up."

"I can't, Brad. I'll be late for English lit."

"This will only take a minute."

Julie turned and leaned against the wall, waiting as Brad shouldered his way through the stream of scurrying students.

"I didn't see you at lunch today. Where were you?" he asked.

"I had the car, so I went off campus."

"All by yourself?"

"I needed a little time alone."

Brad's blue eyes were worried. "Are you all right? Is everything okay with you?"

"Look, Brad, I can't talk now. I don't want to be late for class."

"Okay, so I'll walk with you. It's just down

39

the hall, and the first bell hasn't even rung yet."

Sighing, Julie gripped her books tightly and began walking again, Brad hovering anxiously at her shoulder.

"It's Tara, isn't it?" he asked.

"What do you mean?"

"Tara's been treating you like dirt the past couple of days. And it's all because of that new guy—Quinn what's-his-name. Isn't it?"

Julie stopped and looked at him in surprise. "What do you know about that?"

Brad shrugged. "I'm not as dumb as I look, Julie. I notice things. Particularly about you. In case you haven't noticed, everything about you interests me."

"Please, Brad—" Julie began.

Brad held up one hand and smiled wryly. "Don't worry, I'm not trying to come on to you or anything. At least not right now. It's just that I don't like to see anybody trying to hurt you, and Tara's been doing a real number on you lately."

The first bell rang.

"I really appreciate your worrying about me, Brad," Julie told him hurriedly. "But everything's okay. Tara's just miffed about . . . something. You know how she gets sometimes."

40

She glanced over at her classroom. Mr. Houghton was standing in the open doorway, one hand on the knob, beckoning to her. He liked to start class right on time, with everyone seated before the second bell.

"I've got to go," she said. "But thanks, Brad. Thanks for worrying. That was sweet of you."

"I'm a real sweet guy. See ya later." Brad tossed her a little two-fingered salute and was gone.

Julie found it hard to keep her mind on what Mr. Houghton was saying, even though he was one of her favorite teachers, and English lit one of her more enjoyable classes.

They were discussing Shakespeare's *Othello*, and the violent jealousy that caused Othello to murder his innocent wife.

I've sure had some firsthand experience of jealousy lately, Julie thought. *Tara knows there's something going on between Quinn and me, and she's burning up with jealousy about it.*

But what *was* going on between her and Quinn?

Nothing . . . and everything.

Julie had read somewhere that just before a tornado the earth gets still and heavily oppressive, as if the oxygen has been sucked out of the air.

That's how it was with her and Quinn. Something was coming. She could feel it.

And so could Tara.

Mentally Julie counted off the days she'd known Quinn: Thursday, that was the first. He'd come to school on Thursday. Then Friday, that was the day he'd touched her hand when he'd taken her tray. She'd thought about him all Saturday and Sunday, walking around in a daze, wondering what he would do on Monday.

Monday was Day Five. Long enough, surely, for him to make his move.

But he hadn't. And not yesterday, Tuesday, either.

It wasn't that he was ignoring her, though.

The term "stalking" came to Julie's mind, but she brushed it aside. And yet wasn't that what he was doing? Stalking her?

No, being stalked was a frightening thing and this wasn't frightening. It was exciting. Thrilling. She loved his looks, the way he moved, everything about him, and she was being consumed by her growing obsession with him. Like an addict, she lived only for her next "fix," her next sight of him.

These past two days, in the halls, she would turn around, feeling his presence, knowing he was there. And she would be right. He'd be behind her—at a short distance, but behind her. A couple of times he'd even accidentally bumped into her, disappearing before she could collect her wits.

It was almost as if there were some sort of extrasensory bond between them. Julie didn't even have to see him now to know when he was there, somewhere, watching her, brooding over her. She could feel his eyes on her . . . on her hair, her body.

How much longer would they drift like this, alone but together? Should she go up to him and speak? No, it wasn't the right time yet. She sensed that he wanted it like this. That it was his way of making himself known to her, courting her. That what was happening between them was too important to rush.

I think this is what I've been waiting for all my life, Julie thought dizzily.

The only thing that clouded her happiness was Tara. Julie didn't know what to do about Tara.

On Monday, Tara had come to school dressed for a manhunt: miniskirt to show off her gorgeous legs, a short, tight sweater, and her hair in the flowing, careless, tousled look that, Julie knew, took Tara hours to achieve. She'd positioned herself by the front entrance to the school that morning, waiting for Quinn.

"Today's the day," she'd told Jessica and Shelley. "That McNeal hunk won't know what hit him."

The three of them laughed together, sharing the joke. Tara was deliberately ignoring Julie, still punishing her for what had happened in the cafeteria on Friday.

"I believe it. You look gorgeous, Tara," Jessica had said admiringly.

Julie had walked up to the trio earlier, trying to act as if nothing were wrong, but was unable to get a conversation going with them. None of them had called her over the weekend, either. They usually spent a lot of time together on the phone as well as at the mall on weekends, but whatever the three of them had done, Julie hadn't been included. And judging from the cold look Shelley gave her Monday morning, she felt the same way as Jessica—that Julie had been disloyal to Tara on Friday.

Julie finally shrugged and moved a short distance away to join a group from her homeroom who were talking about current movies.

Out of the corner of her eye, she watched as Tara reached in her shoulder bag and pulled out a tube of lipstick. She smeared it on her lips without using a mirror. Julie had never figured out how she did it.

"Oooh, that's a sexy color," Shelley said approvingly.

"Crimson Passion," Tara said with a knowing wink. "Nick says it's a real turn-on."

"What about Nick?" Jessica asked. "If you drop him for Quinn, he's really going to be hurt."

"Well, those are the breaks of the game, aren't they?" Tara replied, running her hands through her hair and shaking it back, readying herself for her first encounter with her intended victim. "All's fair in love and war."

And then Quinn had treated her, the fabulously beautiful and desirable Tara Braxton, like a fly on the wall!

When Quinn walked up the stairs, she'd turned the full wattage of her cheerleader smile on him, but he didn't seem to notice.

Then she'd dropped her books right in his path.

Without saying a word Quinn had stooped,

picked up the books, and handed them to her.

"Thank you," she'd said in her most seductive voice. "I'm such a klutz!"

He'd smiled slightly, then started to move off, up the stairs and into the building.

Tara sidestepped toward him. Then, prettily, in pretended confusion, moved with him as he tried to go around her.

For a few seconds they seemed to be doing a bizarre little tango.

This was Quinn's chance to say something. A come-on line. Something—anything—that would be the start of that Something Big that Tara had in mind.

Instead, smiling politely, Quinn took hold of Tara's shoulders and moved around her and up the stairs.

Julie witnessed the entire performance. She saw Tara's jaw drop slightly and her cheeks flush with anger—saw Tara toss her head and try to laugh off what had happened, then turn and say something under her breath to Shelley and Jess.

They laughed dutifully, looking a little bewildered.

And then Quinn had turned and looked over at Julie. Looked at her long and hard, the kind of look that made her legs buckle slightly at the knees.

There was no mistaking that look.

Quinn was showing who he was interested in, making it clear that it definitely wasn't Tara.

Tara saw it, and her face turned an unbecoming mottled shade of red and white.

And Julie had known that she was the one who would have to pay the price for Tara's humiliation.

She'd been right. Her relationship with Tara had tobogganed madly downhill from that moment.

And as she'd expected, Shelley and Jessica took Tara's part.

Tara knew a hundred different ways of snubbing someone, and she used at least a dozen of them on Julie in the two days following the big meeting-Quinn-McNeal disaster.

She started right away, at lunch on Monday.

"Shelley, Jess," she'd said loudly, making sure Julie was listening. "Let's go to the mall after school. We can meet Nick and some of the guys later for pizza."

No mention of Julie. When Jessica looked over at Julie questioningly, Tara had said, "Oh, I'm sure Julie will be busy with homework. You know how hard she has to work to make the honor roll."

In a detached way Julie felt sorry for Tara. Most of the upperclassmen had been standing around watching when Quinn had walked past her, ignoring her charms. It must have been a major embarrassment for someone like Tara, not that she was going to admit it to anyone.

"Maybe he had something else on his mind," Julie heard Shelley tell Tara later that afternoon. "You know, like maybe he was depressed or worried or something."

Julie was in a back booth of the girls' room. Tara, Jess, and Shelley were at the sink. Otherwise, the room was empty. They evidently thought they were alone, judging from the frankness of their discussion.

"Yeah, he had something else on his mind, all right," Tara said grimly. "Sweet little Julie Hagan, from the looks of it. Who ever would have expected someone like *her* to make a play for a guy like that? Especially after I made it clear *I* wanted him."

"Maybe she wasn't making a play for him," Jessica said. "I mean, she was just standing there and . . ."

Tara laughed. It wasn't her usual tinkling,

melodious laugh. "She's making a play for him, trust me. I can tell. I knew she was interested in him that very first day. She was all blushes, remember? Besides, she's been acting kind of funny lately, anyway."

"She *has* been a little distant or something ever since school started," Shelley said. "But I don't think she's been trying to get to Quinn behind your back, Tara. I mean, she's one of *us*!"

"Maybe it's not her fault that Quinn is interested in her," suggested Jessica.

"Believe me," Tara said, "if Quinn is interested in her, she's been doing something underhanded to get his attention."

"That doesn't sound like Julie, though," Jessica said doubtfully.

"Oh, yeah?" retorted Tara.

"But what should we do about it?" Shelley asked. "Should we talk to her or what?"

"No. We'll just play it cool for now—we don't want the whole school gossiping about us. We won't be too obvious about how we feel about her, but we won't be too chummy, either. If Julie thinks she can steal Quinn McNeal from me, she's got another thing coming."

"What do you mean?" Shelley said.

"I mean I'm going to give him another

chance. I always get every guy I go after, and I will this time, too. I want Quinn McNeal and I intend to have him!"

Her voice was flat and hard.

"But how?" Jessica asked. "Quinn isn't like all the other guys here. He seems older. More sophisticated."

Julie, in her booth, could hear water running as Tara concentrated on a plan of attack.

Then the sound of the towel dispenser coughing up a couple of towels.

"I think it's time I threw a party," Tara said slowly. "When in doubt, throw a party."

"A party?" Jessica said. "You mean, at your house?"

"Where else? Listen, don't you think that if he sees me on my home turf, he'll forget all about Julie Hagan?"

"He ought to," Shelley said. "Your home turf is pretty impressive."

"I don't think he realizes just who you are, Tara," Jessica agreed. "I mean, you're not some little nobody from nowhere, you know. So when's the party?"

"As soon as possible. This weekend, if I can set it up."

"Are you going to invite Julie?"

Tara barked a laugh. "Do I have any choice? If I don't, people will talk. After all, we've been friends for years, haven't we? The last thing I want is anyone feeling sorry for Julie."

Julie, in her booth, didn't dare make a sound. If those three knew she'd overheard what they were saying, she'd be in bigger trouble than she was already. She hoped they'd leave soon. How much more could they possibly do to their faces and hair?

The class bell rang. Julie heard them leave. When she felt it was safe to follow, she slipped out of the room and ran down the hall to class.

The next couple of days were hard for Julie. She wasn't good at lying, yet she had to walk around looking happy and normal, in spite of Tara's little underhanded put-downs—the raised eyebrow and slight sneer whenever Julie said something, the shoulder turned to her, shutting her out of the group, the glances exchanged with Jess and Shelley that indicated they were sharing something that didn't include Julie.

She tried talking to Shelley about what was happening, but Shelley only said, "I really can't talk about it now, Julie. I need some distance from it, you know? Maybe we can go into this another time."

And Jessica was even worse. "You really let Tara down," she repeated stubbornly, in spite of Julie's protests that she had done nothing to make Quinn ignore Tara. "And after all Tara's done for you, too!"

And in the meantime Julie was being frozen out of the old foursome.

Mollie was the only person she was able to confide in.

Mollie was her usual optimistic self. "Hang in there, Julie. Tara will settle down after a while. You know her. When she sees that Quinn isn't interested in her—and he certainly doesn't seem to be—she'll find somebody else, or she'll decide Nick's the one she wants after all."

Quinn didn't come to school on Wednesday. He'd been out for half a day Tuesday, too. Julie wondered about him, hoping he wasn't sick, yet she was glad he wasn't there to see her being cold-shouldered by Tara. And she was glad she didn't have to watch Tara coming on to him again, either.

What if Tara's right? she asked herself. *What if she does succeed in getting Quinn interested in her?*

How will I be able to handle something like that?

The thought made her almost sick. Again, she was surprised at the intensity of her feelings for Quinn. And they hadn't even really met or spoken to each other yet!

Today, Wednesday, she'd borrowed her mother's car and driven off campus for lunch, glad to get away from Tara's pettiness.

Brad had noticed. Brad knew what was happening. How many others did?

And how much more of this can I take? she wondered.

Quinn was still absent on Thursday. Julie began to worry about him, but was relieved to see him turn up at school Friday morning.

So, obviously, was Tara. If he wasn't available for her party, all her plans would go down the tube.

She'd been running around all morning, inviting everybody on her list of "eligibles" to her house on Saturday night.

Julie wondered when Tara would get around to inviting her, and she'd been debating whether or not she should accept.

She knew that if she didn't, there would be a lot of gossip around school. If people were beginning to notice the big chill between her and Tara, this would confirm it. And she wasn't ready for that yet.

If she went and had a terrible time, so what? She'd go, put in a couple of hours, and leave. No big deal. At least Brad would be glad to see her.

When Tara finally came up to her and, pretending they were still good friends, told Julie about the party, Julie accepted.

"Yeah. Sounds good, Tara. What time?"

"Seven," Tara replied. "The usual."

"Great!" Julie said, trying to sound enthusiastic. "I'll be there."

And if Quinn's there, too, she wondered, *will he finally talk to me? What can I say to make him think I'm as interesting as he seems to think I am?*

And what will Tara do to me if I succeed?

CHAPTER SEVEN

He hadn't realized his absence from school would be that obvious.

No problem. He'd told his landlady, Mrs. Landon, he was sick, hadn't he? And she'd backed him up to the police. And she would again, in the highly unlikely event the police came around a second time, asking questions.

Yes, on Wednesday he told her he had one of those stomach bug things, said he'd come down with it on Tuesday afternoon, had to come home from school, even, and that it didn't seem to be going away. Right away she'd brought him down a big pot of chicken soup. Nice lady, but a lousy cook. Terrible soup. He'd thrown it down the garbage disposal after she left. But still, she'd be able to swear in court, if it ever came to that,

that he's been sick and she'd ministered to him.

And she was absentminded, too, and suggestible. When he asked her if he'd been playing his TV a little too loudly on Tuesday afternoon, she said yes, maybe he had . . . not that it bothered her, but he ought to have been sleeping, not watching TV, sick as he was.

He hadn't had his TV on at all. He'd just asked her that, planted the idea in her head, so that she'd say, "Yes, that nice Quinn McNeal was in his apartment on Tuesday afternoon. I heard him moving around, watching his TV."

He'd realized everyone knew he was missing from school when that black-haired witch, Tara, practically attacked him Friday morning, all smiles.

She was throwing a party, she said, and she wanted him to come. Wanted him to come to her charming old antebellum mansion—it even had a name, Maywood—for a party on Saturday night. Just her, him, and the cream of Braxton Falls society.

But Julie would be there. He knew she'd be there, so he'd accepted.

Tara had seemed relieved when he said he'd come. You'd almost think she'd planned the party around him. Maybe she had. She sure was trying to come on to him. Did she really think he'd be interested in a shallow flirt like her?

Well, that didn't matter. He was going anyway. What a laugh. He, Quinn McNeal, partying in a mansion with all those snobby little rich kids. Things sure had changed since Alison.

Alison's friends had thought he was scum. Treated him like scum.

So why wasn't he scum now? Maybe because his father, Daddy Dearest, was dead. They didn't know anything about Quinn's father, but his death was going to help Quinn anyway.

Funny, wasn't it? The only decent thing his father had ever done for him was tumble down those stairs so neatly and break his neck.

What a shame this hadn't happened four years ago, when Quinn had been so violently, passionately, in love with Alison. It would have made for one less enemy, one less abuser, at least.

But now his father was dead, and for the first time, he'd actually done something constructive for Quinn. All those years of abuse and drunkenness . . . and to think that now he, Quinn, was heir to a piece of fairly valuable property in Middledale, a small town nearly seventy miles west of Braxton Falls.

The town was spreading. There was talk of a mall. A real-estate developer had been quietly approaching the home owners in Dad's run-down neighborhood. Most of them had sold, and for a good price, but his fool of a father had turned the man down flat. Quinn couldn't understand why. Maybe his brain had turned to mush from all that drinking.

But now Quinn would be able to sell the house. Get a good hunk of cash for it, too.

When he'd met Julie, he knew right away he'd be needing some money. She was special. Classy.

At the present time he was working four, sometimes five evenings a week delivering pizzas, making only enough to meet his everyday expenses. The sale of the house, when it came through, would give him a decent income. He could quit his job at the pizza parlor.

A girl like Julie needed to be taken places, nice places. Expensive places. Besides, if he had to work nights, some other guy might move in on her. That blue-eyed guy in the cafeteria, for example. He didn't want her having anything more to do with that bunch of phonies. As soon as she was his, he was going to see to it she didn't run with that crowd anymore.

So far, everything was working out nicely for him.

At least he hoped so.

The Middledale police, though, had come snooping around.

That's where he'd been Thursday. The Middledale police station.

They'd called him Thursday morning and told him about his father's death and asked him to come in for questioning.

Neighbors had found his father's body Wednesday afternoon, all crumpled up at the bottom of the staircase in the front hall. The police said he'd been dead about twenty-four hours.

Accidental deaths, they told him, had to be investigated. Quinn's father was being held in the local morgue, with an identification tag hanging around one dirty big toe.

"Yes, that's my father," Quinn had told them.

Of course, they wanted to know when Quinn had seen him last. They hinted that it appeared his father had fallen down the stairs with a force not commensurate—that was the word they used—with a simple fall. That maybe he'd been violently pushed.

"Your father's neighbors say the two of you

never got along," said the fat-faced sergeant in charge of the investigation. "So can you tell us where you were on Tuesday afternoon?"

"I was sick in bed in the basement apartment I rent in Braxton Falls," he told them. "Ask my landlady. She can vouch for me.

Mrs. Landon had come through for him, the old sweetheart, just as he'd known she would. So he was in the clear, and the police seemed satisfied that the death was, in fact, accidental.

Well, no wonder. The death fit the conventional pattern, didn't it? Every town had its local drunk. And what could be more natural or predictable than this colorful character, the town drunk, falling to his death one day down a long, steep flight of stairs?

He'd made arrangements with a funeral director for his father's cremation.

"No, I don't want the ashes. And no service, please. My father didn't have any friends and often told me he didn't want any kind of burial ceremony."

That wasn't what his father had really wanted, but what difference did it make? He was gone forever, and what he wanted didn't matter now.

Quinn was free. Free of his father and the miserable past. And soon he'd have enough money to compete with those snobby rich guys who were always coming on to Julie.

He'd go to that party on Saturday night, and when the time was right, the moment absolutely perfect, he'd get Julie alone and tell her what she meant to him.

And then she'd tell him she loved him, too.

CHAPTER EIGHT

When Julie arrived at Maywood Saturday night, the party was in full swing, judging by the number of cars in the driveway. She had to park down by the tall wrought-iron gates at the entrance to the broad circular drive and make her way up a slight incline to the front door, careful of her heels in the crushed gravel.

The wide marble foyer was lit by a huge, glittering crystal chandelier that hung down from an upper floor. Wanda, the Braxtons' maid, directed Julie downstairs to the entertainment area.

As she went down the winding, carpeted stairs, Julie marveled at the enormous effort and expense that must have gone into restoring and redoing an old plantation house like this.

To her left was the games room. Julie wandered in and looked around. No sign of Tara . . . or Quinn.

A huge antique pool table with massive carved legs stood in the middle of the room with a triple-width Tiffany-style lamp suspended over it. A couple of guys from the football team were intent over a cutthroat game of pool and didn't look up as she passed them.

Over in a corner a small group, cheered on by Lisa Doyle and a couple of other pom-pom girls, were playing electronic games.

Brad's head surfaced and he grinned.

"Hey, Julie! Over here!"

Julie smiled and shook her head slightly. This was not the night to get clutched to the side of Brad Stafford.

French doors in the games room led out to a half-enclosed deck, but the doors were shut. Julie walked over and looked out.

A large, luxurious hot tub sat in the middle of the deck. It was cold. No steam was rising from its depths.

The Braxtons had been the first family in town to get a hot tub. In an uptight little burg like Braxton Falls, hot tubs were initially viewed with distrust and considered suspiciously decadent, although Mrs. Braxton went around telling people that it was doing wonderful things for her arthritis.

Tara had a few other tales about the uses of a hot tub, but Julie never stayed around to listen to them. Tara exaggerated a lot, anyway.

"Don't be such a prude, Julie," Tara had called once to Julie's rigid, retreating back. "What's wrong with skinny-dipping? You can't see anything. You're under all those bubbles!"

Across the hall from the games room was the family room, if you could call something that vast and luxurious a family room. Julie wandered into the dimly lit room and looked around.

Soft music, old-fashioned cheek-to-cheek dance music, was playing, and some of the Oriental throw rugs had been moved to the side of the room. Several couples were in the middle of the floor, heads together, swaying dreamily to the music. . . .

Jessica was there with Thad Turner, a freshman at college who was home for the weekend. They'd been an "item" since last summer. According to Jessica, it was the real thing.

Well, good luck, Jessica, Julie thought. *I hope you're right. Maybe dating a college guy will help get you out from under Tara's thumb.*

Shelley Molino was dancing with Colin King. The two of them seemed to be getting together more and more often these days. Shelley looked over at Julie but didn't wave and smile at her, the way she would have two weeks ago.

That hurt a little. Julie had to remind herself that Shelley wasn't mean, just weak, and was easily led around by Tara.

Shelley and everyone else I know, Julie thought.

She heard Tara before she saw her. Even over the music, Tara's wild soprano laugh stood out.

She was over in a corner, surrounded by a group of people, mostly guys. The turquoise silk outfit she was wearing—plunging vee-necked crop top and palazzo pants—lit up her part of the room.

Julie realized immediately that Tara was playing to an audience, and it wasn't those cute jocks and student-body leaders clustered around her, either.

Sure enough, there was Quinn.

He was sitting in a dark corner opposite Tara, but he wasn't looking at her. As far as Julie could see from the bored, slightly cynical expression on his face, Tara was playing to an empty house.

Then Quinn looked up and saw Julie. His eyes widened, and he leaned forward in his chair.

Julie felt the warm blood rise in her cheeks.

Get up. Come over here. Talk to me, she willed.

"Look, everybody, here's Julie," Tara called out. "And doesn't she look sweet!"

There was a chorus of "Hi, Julie" all around. Julie nodded back and then glanced over at Quinn.

The mood of the moment had been shattered. Quinn had sunk back in his chair, his face unreadable, nursing his cola. A sour, bitter anger replaced the aching tenderness Julie had felt for him just a brief moment ago.

I'm getting tired of this, she thought suddenly. *What's he up to, anyway? If he's as interested in me as he's pretending to be with those long, brooding looks, then why hasn't he done something about it?*

And suddenly Julie realized she'd had too much.

Too much of Tara and her nastiness. Too much of Quinn with his silent, eternal, devastating stare.

She'd been hoping tonight would be the night. That Quinn would finally do something to break the ice—talk to her, ask her out, something!

She turned on her heel and left the room. Brad was out in the hall. He tried to say something to her, tried to take hold of her arm, but she brushed him off and kept going.

Up the stairs, hitting every tread, wishing it were Tara. Or Quinn.

A minute to get Wanda to help find her purse, and then out into the night.

The wind had picked up a bit and was blowing fluttering rags of clouds across a fat yellow moon.

Julie walked quickly down the driveway to her car, not caring if the gravel chewed the suede off the heels of her shoes.

She was just opening her door when she heard a light, firm tread behind her.

She knew who it was.

She turned, not knowing what to say or do.

And then, smiling, Quinn McNeal came to her through the moonlight.

Up close, under the streetlight, Julie saw that Quinn's eyes weren't as dark as she'd thought. They'd appeared almost black from afar.

"Why, your eyes are blue . . . dark blue," she said softly, reaching out and gently touching his cheek with her fingertip.

It was an involuntary gesture that she regretted immediately.

Why on earth did I have to go and say that? she asked herself incredulously.

She dropped her hand and blushed furiously. *What a stupid thing to say . . . and do,* she thought.

But Quinn, still looking at her, reached down and took her hand, holding her palm against his warm, rough cheek.

Julie was surprised to feel his hand tremble.

A sudden gust of wind blew her long hair against his face.

And then he kissed her. He drew her close against him and kissed her again. And again.

He released her and ran his hands down her arms.

Julie was shocked at her physical response to his kiss, his touch.

He cleared his throat.

"Look . . . Julie," he began. He seemed to linger over her name. "This probably sounds crazy, but—"

Other footsteps on the gravel. Other shadows between them and the moon. Julie was suddenly aware that they were not alone.

CHAPTER NINE

Two figures materialized in the darkness beside them.

A prickle of fear ran down Julie's back. There was something menacing, threatening, about the way they stood, shoulder to shoulder.

Julie could see their faces in the moonlight. Strangers, both of them. No one she had ever seen at Jefferson High. They were older, too, and certainly not the type Tara would invite to one of her parties.

Maybe they're only harmless party crashers, she told herself as she waited for them to speak. But Julie knew they were more than that. There was nothing harmless about these two.

Quinn seemed to sense it, too.

"What do you guys want?" he asked. His

voice was mild, but Julie could feel his body grow tense, his muscles tighten. He took his arm from her shoulder and moved away from her, a step to the side, as he spoke.

"Now what do you think we want?" sneered the bigger of the two. "What would little rich kids who like to party have that some poor guy like me would want?"

"Please," Julie said. "If it's money you're after . . ." She held her handbag out to them.

"I'll take care of this, Julie," Quinn said.

"Oooh, so it's Julie," the other stranger said. Then, in a mocking falsetto, "Isn't that sweet, Norm? Her name is Julie. Can I have her when you're done with Mr. Wonderful here?"

"Sure, Frankie, she's just your type. I think she's got the hots for you already," Norm replied. "Isn't that right, Julie?" He made kissing noises at her.

Then, before Julie had time to realize what was happening, Quinn moved. His foot lashed out, catching Norm in the groin. As Norm doubled over, grunting and clutching at his stomach, Quinn, his fists joined, hit him hard on the back of his neck.

Norm fell to the ground, moaning, and Quinn turned to Frankie, who'd been watching, too startled to move.

"Now it's your turn," he said in a low, harsh voice.

He grabbed Frankie by the wrist, spinning him around to twist his arm up behind him at an unnatural angle. Then he kneed him sharply in the back, yanking his arm up even higher as Frankie's back arched in pain.

Julie heard a loud snap followed by a muffled scream from Frankie. Muffled because Quinn had thrown his other arm around Frankie's throat, throttling him.

That snap! Was it a bone breaking?

Julie gasped. Oh, God, this was terrible. Quinn was going to kill him!

"Please, Quinn! That's enough!" she whispered.

On the ground Norm began to move, to crawl sideways, like a crab.

Without releasing his hold on Frankie, Quinn pivoted slightly and kicked Norm in the ribs. Then he kicked him again, harder this time.

Norm sprawled out full length, sobbing.

Quinn laughed softly. He seemed to be enjoying what he was doing. Julie almost didn't recognize his face in the moonlight. It was twisted. Cruel.

He raised his foot to kick Norm again.

Terrified now, Julie lunged at Quinn and grabbed him. "Stop it! Stop it, Quinn! Please!" she sobbed.

Quinn turned and looked at her. The expression on his face cleared. He looked almost puzzled.

"And what do you think they would have done to you, Julie, if I hadn't been here?"

Frankie was crying now, silently. Tears of pain streamed down his cheeks. His nose ran, as if someone had turned on a spigot. He bent over, writhing in Quinn's grasp.

Quinn looked down at him in disgust. Then he released him, pushing him away with a quick, violent motion.

"You're not so tough now, are you, creep?" he snarled.

Frankie stumbled and nearly fell, but managed to catch himself before he did. His arm—even his shoulder—was hanging oddly.

"Quinn, I'm going to run back to the house and call the police."

"No!" he yelled. "No police."

"Please, girl, get the police," Norm moaned, clutching his ribs. "This guy is trying to kill us."

"Do you hear me, Julie? No police," Quinn told her. "I'd rather settle this myself."

Yanking the sobbing, trembling Norm to his feet, he demanded, "Where's your car?"

Norm didn't reply. He shrank away from him in terror, as if afraid Quinn would hit him again.

Quinn shook him. "Answer me. Where's your car?"

"Over there," Norm moaned, pointing. "Just outside the gates."

Quinn roughly dragged Norm and Frankie toward the battered Ford Escort they said was their car. Frankie was sagging, clearly almost fainting from the pain in his shoulder, and Quinn had to bear him up with one arm as he pulled him and Norm along.

Julie, following behind, marveled at his strength. Quinn was tall, but lean. *He must be all muscle*, she thought numbly.

Before thrusting Frankie and Norm into the car, Quinn shoved them against the hood and barked: "Hand over your wallets!"

"Sure, guy," Norm said. "Take them. There's not much money, but—"

"I don't want your money, just your driver's licenses."

Quinn had to reach into Frankie's pocket for

him—Frankie's shoulder was in pretty bad shape.

Quinn quickly removed the licenses and tossed the wallets onto the backseat. And then, in a voice that frightened Julie even more, he said, "I know who you are now."

He slapped their licenses against his open palm. "I know who you are now," he repeated. "And no matter where you go, I have ways of finding you if I need to. So I don't want you to give me any reason for tracking you down, okay?"

"Okay, okay, man!"

"What I'm saying is, I don't want to see either of you again, or hear of you, or have any reason to even suspect you're still alive, stinking up the world. Do you understand? Do you know what I'm saying?"

"We get you, man. Hey, we're out of here. For good. That's a promise, man!" said Norm.

"Yeah! That's right!" put in Frankie.

Quinn's voice became even more deadly. More menacing.

"And if either one of you ever comes near Julie again," he said between clenched teeth, "comes *anywhere* near her . . . I'll kill *you*."

CHAPTER TEN

Julie was still trembling long after Norm and Frankie peeled off down the street, laying a strip of rubber in their haste to escape.

All she knew was that she had to get away from that place, away from what had just happened.

"Are you okay, Julie?"

"I'll be all right in a minute."

Wordlessly, Quinn put her in her car and slipped into the driver's seat beside her.

"But what about your car?" Julie protested. "You can't just leave it here overnight."

"I'll walk back later and get it, after I take you home. It's not that far."

"You . . . you know where I live?"

"I know a lot of things about you, Julie."

Quinn started the engine and drove out through Maywood's massive gates. Then he turned left and headed down the hill past the luxurious homes of Hunter Valley.

He drove quickly and directly to Julie's house and pulled into the driveway.

He's been here before, she told herself silently. *Did he come here at night, watching me the way he did at school?* The thought unsettled Julie for a moment. *He probably only came by to check out my address*, she decided.

Besides, that wasn't important now. All that mattered was that he was here, sitting next to her, his face only inches from hers. He kissed her gently, lingeringly, savoring her lips.

She loved the shape of his face, the sharp, clean line of his jaw and chin.

"I found out where you lived that very first day," Quinn confessed.

"You did? How?"

"That girl in the office, Karen Slack. She gave me your address."

"That's weird, Quinn. Karen's really boy crazy. I can't imagine her doing a Cupid act for someone else."

"Oh, it was definitely not a Cupid act," Quinn said, laughing. "I told her I found a dent in the side of my car and I was sure you were the one who did it. I said I wanted to come by your house and bring you to justice."

"But I didn't drive to school that day!"

"Well, she didn't know that," Quinn said. "But enough about Karen Slack." He moved closer to Julie, murmuring something about how beautiful she was and touching her hair—he seemed fascinated by her hair—twining a long strand around his finger and tenderly tucking a stray curl behind her ear.

"I love your hair," he said. "I've always loved your hair."

"Always?" Julie asked. "Like forever? Quinn, do you have the feeling we've known each other before . . . somewhere else . . . in another time? I'm beginning to think I do."

Quinn pulled away from her, his blue eyes darkening and his mouth tightening.

"No, Julie, don't say that," he commanded. "We're starting out new, you and I. It's like getting a second chance at life."

Julie was a little surprised at his reaction. And yet, there were so many surprising things about Quinn.

She was amazed by the depth of feeling he seemed to have for her. She'd never inspired such powerful feelings before in any of the boys she'd been involved with. Was it because he was more experienced and mature than other guys his age? And what made him that way?

There was so much she wanted to learn about him.

"We could go inside," she suggested.

"No," he said, reaching for her again. "I like it here. I like looking at you in the moonlight. But what will your folks think, you parked out here with a stranger?"

"They're at a country-club dance. They won't be home for hours."

Julie's voice quivered a bit at that last word. The thought of staying here for hours with Quinn, touching him, kissing him, took her breath away.

He smiled, as if he could guess what she was thinking.

To cover her embarrassment, she said as matter-of-factly as she could, "You know, Quinn, I don't know anything about you. Nobody does."

"There's not much to know," he said, turning slightly and laying his head back on the headrest.

"Your folks," Julie prompted. "Someone said you're an orphan."

"My mother left my father and me when I was a baby."

"Oh, Quinn, that's terrible!"

"I can't say I blame her, Julie. My father was a drunk and a bully. When I was little, though, and Dad was beating on me, I used to hate her for not loving me enough to stick around and protect me."

"My God, Quinn, your father used to beat you?"

Quinn nodded. His eyes seemed cold. Distant. "It happens all the time, child abuse. Now they're trying to do something about it. Telling kids what to do, who to tell about it. Nobody told me what to do when I was little, though. I thought I was supposed to take it and not say anything."

"What about your father now?" Julie asked. "Is he . . . is he sorry for what he did?"

"I hope he's paying for it this very minute," Quinn said fiercely.

Then, glancing at Julie's shocked expression, he said, "He died on Tuesday. Fell down a flight of stairs when he'd been drinking and broke his neck."

Quinn didn't seem at all sorry, and Julie didn't blame him. Still, she couldn't help being surprised.

"This past Tuesday?" she asked. "Then that was why you were absent from school?"

"Actually, no. I had the flu Tuesday and Wednesday. The police came and told me about Dad on Thursday. That's why I didn't come to school that day, although I was okay by then. It's a good thing, too. I had to go to Middledale—that's where my father lived—and . . . and claim his body."

"And you haven't said a word, not one word, about it to anyone?" Julie was aghast. So much had happened to Quinn, her own darling Quinn, and yet he didn't go around complaining or looking for pity. She couldn't understand him.

"Besides making arrangements for what they call the 'disposition of the remains,'" Quinn said, "I talked to a realtor about selling Dad's house. It's the only thing he left me. It's not much, but the land is being zoned for a mall. I think I can get enough out of it to live comfortably for a while. And now I can quit my pizza-delivery job. It's been a real drag."

"I didn't know you delivered pizza," Julie exclaimed. "I wish I'd known. I would have ordered one every night."

Quinn laughed. "I come by here all the time.

I've seen you through your front window a couple of times. I'd pull over and watch you."

He stopped, sat up, and pulled her to him.

"Julie, if you only knew how I'd sit there, looking at you, wanting to do this."

Julie felt groggy when she emerged from his embrace. That was the only word for it. Groggy.

Quinn released her guiltily, hastily, as if he'd gone too far.

There was an old-fashioned streak about him, Julie decided fondly from the depth of her daze. A cavalier, that's what he was. Or maybe a knight in shining armor?

She shook her head slightly, to fight off the delicious, sinking sensation she seemed to feel now that she was—at long last!—in Quinn's arms.

Quinn turned again, his hands on the steering wheel, his breathing calm.

"Well, anyway, I'd take Grady with me on my deliveries. Old Grady would paw at me when we parked too long, looking in your window."

"Grady? Who's he?"

"My cat."

There was an unmistakable tone of pride in Quinn's voice when he said that.

"You have a cat?" Julie asked.

Now *here* was a facet of Quinn's life Julie would never have guessed at. Quinn, a cat person?

"Yeah, he's kind of old and crotchety, but we belong together," Quinn said.

He went on to tell Julie how he'd found Grady wet, muddy, and furiously angry, in a ditch.

"He'd obviously been abandoned," Quinn said. "Probably thrown from a car. I couldn't help admiring Grady for the way he was taking it."

"Oh?" Julie said, amused by Quinn's obvious love for his pet.

"Yeah," Quinn said. "Grady was spitting mad. I got a few scratches and bites trying to get him out of the ditch. But now we're best friends." Quinn smiled at Julie.

"People say cats are independent and unfeeling," he continued. "But that's not true. They really get attached to you."

It had started to rain—a thin, cold drizzle that clouded the windows. Julie felt cut off, isolated from the rest of the world, and she wished they could stay that way forever.

Quinn reached out and drew two entwined hearts on the misty window. He added an arrow and their initials, and smiled sheepishly at her.

"I've been waiting to do that," he said. "That makes us official, okay?"

Julie ran her finger gently along the thin scar that bisected his upper lip. "Somebody said you were in an accident and lost a year of school. Is that where you got this?"

"It wasn't an accident exactly," he said brusquely. "But I *have* been away. And I did lose a year of school. My past three years were . . . well . . . kind of private tutoring, you might say."

There were so many things Julie wanted to ask Quinn about himself. So many questions.

But when he drew her to him again and their lips met, she forgot everything else.

CHAPTER ELEVEN

I kissed her, he thought joyfully. *I held her and kissed her and I know, by the way she responded, the way she clung to me and kissed me back, that she loves me too.*

She loves me as much as I love her. No . . . maybe not as much as that. Not yet. She couldn't possibly love me that much already. But she will. In time. I'll teach her to make me her whole world, just as she is mine.

He picked up Grady, who was rubbing against his ankles, nuzzled him lovingly, and carried him into the small alcove that served as a bedroom.

He tossed the cat onto the bed, threw off his clothes, and crawled between the sheets.

She loves me.

Alison loves me.

No . . . wait a minute. It's Julie, not Alison.

Alison is . . . gone. Gone forever. I saw her lying

there, white and bloodless. Mustn't think of Alison.

Julie's the one I love. And isn't she beautiful? That long, silken hair, just like Alison's. No! Not like Alison's! Forget Alison. Think only of Julie. I love Julie. Julie! Julie is sweet and lovely and good. She'd never try to trick me and make a fool of me the way . . .

No, Julie would never betray me. She loves me and I love her. It's different this time.

And tonight I saved her. I was there for her and I saved Julie from those two. I know what they wanted. It wasn't her purse, her money. No. They wanted to do terrible things to her, to throw her down on the ground and . . . but I was there. And I knew what to do.

Yes, I knew what to do. I learned how to fight in The Place. I was a dumb kid when I went in there, but I learned fast. I had to.

But those two. That Norm and Frankie. Yes, they said they wouldn't come back, but I know their type. They would never come back again for me, but they'll want revenge. Revenge for what I did to them. The shame I inflicted on them.

And so they'll get revenge on me by hurting Julie. They'll find her and trail her, and then . . . No. I will never allow that to happen.

Those two are scum.

They shouldn't be allowed to live.

CHAPTER TWELVE

The next morning Julie resolved not to tell her parents, or anyone, about what had happened in the driveway of Tara's house.

"Don't, Julie," Quinn had warned her in the car the night before. "If we get involved, we'll have to fill out police reports and answer questions. And they'll be calling us down to the station every time there's a robbery or a purse snatching. Besides," he'd argued, "I took care of the problem, didn't I? We'll never see those two again."

Julie shuddered, remembering Frankie and what he might have done to her if Quinn hadn't been there.

"But what if they *do* come back?" she'd asked. "Those two were mean. Really mean,

Quinn. Maybe they'll think it over and decide to get revenge."

"No. No, they won't." Quinn's face was closed, unreadable. "Trust me."

But now Julie remembered another look on Quinn's face—the look he'd worn when he was beating up on the two muggers.

He'd looked almost as if he were enjoying it.

No, that can't be true, Julie thought. After all, she had been half out of her head with fear at the time. Surely she'd imagined it. Quinn was saving her, wasn't he? How many guys did she know who could have handled the situation the way he had?

Mollie obviously sensed, the minute Julie sat down at the Sunday breakfast table, that something big had happened to Julie the night before.

"How was Tara's party?" Mollie asked casually for the benefit of their parents, but flashing her sister a secret and urgent questioning look,

"Oh, that's right, Julie," her mother said, looking up from the stove where she was scrambling eggs. "How was the party? Did you have a nice time?"

Julie arranged crisp, drained slices of bacon

on a large blue-and-white platter and held it out while her mother spooned the eggs onto it.

"Yes, I did," she replied, attempting to sound matter-of-fact. "And I met—I mean, I really got to know—this cute new guy at school. His name's Quinn McNeal."

Mollie flashed her a discreet thumbs-up.

Julie could feel her cheeks redden and a dopey grin spread across her face at the mention of Quinn's name.

Fortunately, her father was buried behind the editorial pages of the paper and her mother's back was to her, or they would have picked up on both the blush and the grin. No one could ever accuse Mr. and Mrs. Hagan of being unconcerned parents. They were always a little *too* concerned in Julie's and Mollie's opinions.

"New boy?" her mother said vaguely, pouring the orange juice and setting the glasses on the table. "I don't recall you mentioning a new boy at school. McNeal, you say? I don't think I've ever met his parents."

Julie tried to smother her annoyance. Why did Mom always have to think in terms of Who's Who in Braxton Falls?

"He doesn't have any parents," she said shortly. "He's an orphan."

Her father put down his paper at that. "An orphan? Does he live with relatives, or what?"

"No, he lives alone in a basement apartment in town. He expects to get a small inheritance from the sale of his father's house, but in the meantime he supports himself by . . ." She paused and drew a deep breath. Her mother wasn't going to like this one. ". . . by delivering pizzas."

Her mother sat down quickly in her chair and eyed Julie shrewdly. "Do you think there's a chance that you and this . . . this McNeal person will be seeing each other socially? Dating, I mean?"

Julie returned her stare. "Yes, Mom, I'd say we're going to be seeing a lot of each other. He's really special. And he seems to think I am, too."

"He's incredibly good-looking," Mollie put in, trying to be helpful. "All the girls are crazy about him. They'll be furious when they find out Julie's got him."

"*Got* him?" her mother said. "You've *got* a pizza-delivery boy?"

Help came from an unexpected quarter.

"Don't be such a snob, Vivian," Mr. Hagan said, laying his newspaper aside and picking up his fork. "He sounds like a nice kid. And for the record, I was hustling hamburgers in a greasy-spoon diner when you *got* me, remember?"

Telling Tara wasn't as bad as Julie had expected.

Tara didn't appear at all surprised or angry at the news that Julie and Quinn were now a couple. She actually seemed pleasant, almost sisterly, about it.

"I've noticed the way he looks at you, Julie," she said affably. "He's got it bad for you. When I saw him leave the party right behind you, I figured he was up to something."

She laughed her trademark melodious laugh and wagged her finger with its long scarlet nail before Julie's face. "Now, you better hang on to him and treat him right, or I'll move in on you, hear? That guy's a real hunk!"

Julie's relief turned sour when she saw Shelley and Jessica share a secret smile at Tara's words. Naturally they were on Tara's side. They always would be.

So what did that nasty little smile mean?

Tara moved off down the hall and Julie turned to Jess and Shelley.

"Look, I hope what's happened between Quinn and me isn't going to change things between us," she said.

Jessica looked uncomfortable and refused to meet Julie's eyes, but Shelley faced her squarely.

"Of course it's going to change things between us, Julie. Why shouldn't it? You didn't play fair with Tara, so why should we trust you? There's nothing lower than a boyfriend stealer. She told us right from the start that she wanted Quinn for herself, but you had to go and cut in on her, didn't you?"

Julie stared at her friend helplessly. "For the last time, Shelley, I didn't *steal* Quinn. You can't steal people. Besides, he never belonged to Tara in the first place. What made her think she owned him?"

"Come on, Jess," Shelley said. "We've got to catch up with Tara."

Julie watched bleakly as the two of them hurried away from her, not looking back.

It was over. Their friendship was over. Julie was sure of it now. Tara would never forgive her as long as she was going with Quinn, and Jess and Shelley would always stick with Tara, no matter what. Shelley was a blind follower, and Jess was too weak to take a stand on anything.

Julie had been critical of them these past few months, but she would still miss them. Miss the things they did together. Miss being part of a charmed circle of four.

She sighed, grasped her books tightly, and headed down the hall to her next class. But just then she saw Quinn coming toward her, shouldering his way through clumps of giggling, chattering teens, and smiling a special smile, just for her.

We're a couple now, she thought, smiling back and moving toward him, forgetting Tara and the others. *I have Quinn and that's all that matters.*

Quinn put his arm around her shoulder and gave her a quick kiss on the top of her head, almost as if he were staking a claim on her for all the world to see.

All around them were astonished eyes and surprised faces, and Julie was aware that everyone was staring at her, and that she probably looked silly and lovestruck.

Well, let them look, she thought happily, kissing him back. *By lunchtime it will be all over school about Quinn and me, anyway. So I might as well relax and let it all hang out.*

Brad Stafford had been one of those standing, watching. He smiled at Julie as she went past with Quinn. It wasn't his usual smile. This was a regretful, almost sad little smile, not at all like Brad.

Quinn was waiting for Julie in the hall outside every classroom that day.

"You don't have to do that, Quinn," she protested. "I don't want you to be late for your own classes."

"But I want to," he said. "I like carrying your books. It makes me feel like one of those old-fashioned boyfriends."

He was missing from his post only once, and that was when Julie came out of world history.

He wasn't far away, though. Boy-crazy Karen Slack had him pinned up against the wall a little way down the hall. She was saying something to him, posing a bit, shaking back her thick, heavily permed hair and smiling an arch, teasing smile.

She seemed to be asking—no, telling—him something. Julie couldn't see Quinn's face when he replied, but when he finally got away from Karen and came toward Julie, he looked annoyed.

"I'm not going to ask what you and Karen were up to," Julie told him, laughing. "I don't want you to accuse me of being jealous of her."

Quinn rolled his eyes. "She was asking me how things worked out between you and me. I mean, about that dent I told her you put in my car. She even volunteered to help me find a good automotive shop where I can get my car fixed."

"I guess she hasn't heard the latest about us, then," Julie said. "She must be the only one in school who hasn't. This place is a real gossip mill."

"There's always one clueless person," Quinn said cheerfully, linking his arm with hers. "And now, Miss Hagan, since I don't have to report for work until late tonight, how about letting me take you out for frozen yogurt after last class?"

CHAPTER THIRTEEN

What was it with these girls at Jefferson High? Why were they all trying to put the make on him? Hadn't he made it clear, right from the start, that the only girl he was interested in was Julie?

First it had been Tara. She'd been attracted to him, he could tell, and she'd tried to make him interested in her, too. Fat chance. She wasn't his kind of girl. He only hoped Tara wasn't going to try to make Julie miserable on his account. She was the kind of girl who'd do something like that. Well, let her try. Julie had *him*, now, and he wasn't about to let anybody hurt her.

And now Karen Slack was hitting on him.

Why did she have to come after him? Didn't

she know he and Julie were a pair, or was she just plain stupid?

The girl was trouble, and he was going to have to do something about her before she ruined his life. No sense trying to kid himself, she had the power to really mess him up.

She'd caught him in the hall today and, acting all cute and flirty, had said, "I know your secret, Quinn McNeal!"

At first he didn't know what she meant. He'd thought maybe she was talking about him and Julie. But then she'd said, "I know where you've been the last four years."

He'd tried to play it cool, to keep a friendly expression on his face. He didn't want anyone wondering what they were saying and listening in.

"What do you mean?" he asked, stalling for time.

"You've got a real interesting past," she said. "No wonder you look so . . . experienced."

Her voice had drifted off but her eyes were bold.

It was funny how some girls were turned on by guys who'd been in The Place. It happened all the time, though, according to a couple of guys who'd been in there before.

But how did Karen know about his past?

Then it hit him. Karen worked in the principal's office. She'd seen his records! How could she have seen them, though? Mr. Reed said he was keeping them locked up in his special safe. The one only he had the combination to.

Mr. Reed was a nice man, an okay guy. He wasn't the sort to betray a trust. You developed a sixth sense about people when you'd been in The Place for a while. You could always tell those you could trust from those you couldn't.

He'd talked to Quinn in his office the day Quinn registered.

"Look, son," he'd said, "what you did is in the past, and you've certainly paid enough for it. It's the future that matters now. So I'm going to put these records and the letters that accompanied them here in my private safe, where only I can have access to them."

Seeing that Quinn was still a little uncertain, Mr. Reed had continued, "Sometimes a high-school principal has to be like a doctor or a priest. There are some things we keep to ourselves."

"But the other teachers," Quinn said. "Won't they have to—"

"No. I'll personally compile your reports. The important thing here, Quinn, is to get you back

97

on the right track, and the less others know about your past, the better."

And now Karen said she knew his secret. How did that happen?

"What is this, Karen?" he'd asked, trying to keep it low-key. "Are you pulling my leg or what?"

She'd smiled and run her hands through her hair. It was an annoying mannerism, Quinn noted, but she obviously thought she looked sexy doing it.

"Mr. Reed's gotten real absent-minded lately," she said. "Would you believe he went off this morning and left his safe wide open? Why, anyone could have gone in and read your records, Quinn."

She smiled again, but a threat lay beneath that smile.

"I closed it up real quick, though," she said. "Of course, I just *might* have glanced at some of the stuff Mr. Reed had in there about you. But don't worry, Quinn. Your secret is safe with me."

Well, at least she hadn't told anyone else . . . yet.

That figured—knowledge was power. And she had the knowledge about his past, so she had power over him. She probably wouldn't want to share it with anyone until she found out what it would buy.

He'd played it cool with her. He pretended he felt friendly toward her and that maybe they could get together and talk about it. Tonight, even. He said he'd call her. That way, even if she heard about him and Julie, she'd figure it was just gossip.

That pizza-delivery job sure made things easier. It gave him an alibi.

He'd call her after school and set up a meeting for tonight.

CHAPTER FOURTEEN

On Tuesday afternoon two policemen found the body of Karen Slack.

Her car was parked a few miles from town at a scenic overlook, a high bluff with a view of the Potomac River and the famous falls for which the town was named.

Her body was lying, spread-eagled, on the rocks below.

The police said she had either jumped, fallen, or been pushed from the overlook at approximately eleven o'clock on Monday night.

Murder, her shocked classmates agreed, was completely out of the question. Who would want to murder Karen Slack?

The police seemed to agree with the students of Jefferson High. They could find no motive for the possible murder of Karen Slack. And her body showed no signs of any injuries other than those caused by the impact of her fall.

That left accident and suicide.

Suicide seemed about as unlikely as murder. The police interviewed Karen's friends and classmates, and no one could remember her ever acting "down" or depressed, or saying anything about wishing she were dead.

"Just the opposite," her best friend, Cassie Latimore, told the police. "She was always disgustingly cheerful. But what I can't figure out is, why did she go up to the overlook? I mean, that's a big parking spot for kids who want to make out, and Karen didn't have anyone to make out with."

"Maybe she just wanted to go up there at night and pretend," suggested Ann Collins, another of Karen's friends. "And you know what a klutz Karen was. She probably leaned over the railing too far, lost her balance, and fell."

Accidental death, the police ruled it, and closed their books on the case.

"I feel so awful about Karen," Julie told Quinn at lunch the next day as they sat in a private, sunny spot down by the gym, sharing sandwiches and cookies.

The two of them were brown-bagging it these days at Quinn's suggestion. He said he didn't like cafeteria food. Julie suspected it was actually the cafeteria and the "in" crowd at the special table he disliked. She was relieved he didn't want to eat with them. It would be awkward to sit there now, considering how Tara, Jess, and Shelley felt about her.

Actually, Quinn acted as if he wanted to keep her away from *everybody*, not just her old friends.

"Why should you feel awful about Karen?" Quinn asked her, polishing an apple on the sleeve of his sweater.

"Well, you know. I feel guilty for not realizing how needy and insecure she must have been. Can you imagine going up to the overlook at night by yourself? I guess no guy ever took her there."

"Are you saying you've been up there, Julie?" Quinn asked. He was smiling, but his eyes were cold. "How many guys have taken you up there?"

"Oh, Quinn, it's not like that at all."

"Who'd you make out with up there? That Brad Stafford creep?"

He reached over and grasped Julie's wrist.

She tried to pull away, but his grip tightened. "I mean it, Julie. I really want to know."

"Let go of me, Quinn!" she gasped. "You're hurting me!"

He didn't seem to hear her. Didn't seem to realize she was in pain. His eyes had darkened. They looked almost black now.

"Who?" he repeated. "Answer me."

"Nobody," Julie said, close to tears. "I've never made out with anybody up on The Point. Now let go of my arm, Quinn."

He loosened his grip on her wrist but didn't remove his hand. "Are you telling me the truth? You've never been with somebody up there?"

Julie tore her arm free and rubbed her wrist. She could see the red imprint of his fingers on it.

"I didn't say I've never been up there," she snapped. "Sure, I've gone up to The Point, but it's always been with a bunch of kids, and we never did anything . . . like that."

She turned and faced him, tears of anger welling up in her eyes. "So listen to me good, Quinn, because I'm not going to say it again. I've never made out with a guy up there. I don't think I've ever actually 'made out'—I mean, well, you know—with anybody anywhere. You're looking at a real inexperienced girl here. So there. Are you satisfied now?"

He stared at her silently for several seconds. She could see his face softening and his eyes losing that wild black look.

"Oh, Julie," he finally said. "I'm sorry. I'm really sorry. I don't know what came over me."

He tried to put his arms around her, but she pulled away.

"No, don't touch me," she commanded. "I don't want you to touch me."

Obediently, he put his hands in his lap and stared bleakly down at them.

"Okay, I won't touch you. But can I say something?"

"What?"

"That I've been a real jerk and I was wrong to act the way I did. It's just that I'm so crazy about you, Julie, it makes me half-nuts sometimes. The thought of you kissing another guy—I mean, parking someplace and really making out with him—nearly drives me wild."

He looked up at her pleadingly. She didn't reply.

"I love you," he repeated. "I guess I'm not showing it the right way, but I do. And I'm sorry I grabbed you like that. Does it hurt?"

"No," Julie told him. "Not now."

"I'll never do anything like that again," he said. "That's a promise."

"Are you sure?"

"Am I sure? Does the sun rise in the east? Do you want me to prove it to you? Ask me to do anything, Julie, and I will. I'll walk on hot coals if you want, just say the word."

"Oh, stop it, dummy," Julie said, smiling in spite of herself. "I forgive you."

Quinn threw out his arms and looked heavenward. "Thank you! Thank you, Lord!"

Later that night, as she lay in bed, Julie thought about what had happened. How jealous Quinn had been. Wild with jealousy.

It was scary to be loved like that. Scary but thrilling. She couldn't believe he felt all that emotion for her. She didn't know any other girl whose boyfriend was that crazy in love with her.

She'd been angry with Quinn when he'd grabbed her wrist and acted so wild, but she couldn't stay mad at him long.

And he'd promised never to do anything like that again, hadn't he?

So everything was okay with them, now.

He had come by after supper and taken her

out to the movies. He'd really impressed her parents.

He'd called her mother "ma'am" and her father "sir." They'd simply eaten it up, her mother in particular. She was always going on about good manners, and how the kids today didn't act respectful around their elders.

Well, Quinn's manners had been perfect, absolutely perfect, and he'd looked like a real Prince Charming in that blue shirt that matched the color of his eyes.

And she could tell that her father was impressed by the fact that Quinn was on his own, earning his own living and going to school at the same time.

When she'd gone upstairs for her purse, Mollie had followed her and said, "Wow, Julie that guy's a walking sexpot. Tara's probably making a wax doll of you this very minute, so be ready for some strange, shooting pains when she starts sticking in the pins."

All in all it had been a very successful first meeting with the folks.

Forget that other stuff at lunch.

It would never happen again.

CHAPTER FIFTEEN

That was a close call at lunch.

He really blew it and nearly lost her for good.

But it wasn't his fault. It was just that he loved her so much.

She shouldn't have talked as if it were natural to go up to The Point. It wasn't. Decent girls didn't do things like that. He was looking for a good girl, someone special, who'd saved herself just for him.

That's why he'd flipped out when Julie started in about The Point. He suddenly got this mental picture of her up there, with some lousy little rich kid's dirty hands all over her.

He hoped she'd never find out just how angry he'd really been. Lucky for him he'd managed to explain it away and make her smile at him again.

He'd liked it when she'd told him she never "made out" with any guy anywhere. What an angel! If she ever changed, he didn't know what he'd do.

Well, he'd been lucky today, all right. Julie's folks really liked him. He could tell. And he had an idea that her father would probably want to take him into the family business if—*when*—he and Julie were married.

That Karen Slack thing had worked out okay, too.

He'd been lucky. The Point was deserted, as he'd hoped it would be, and the whole thing took only a few minutes.

He had no regrets for what he did. After all, it was entirely Karen's fault. She hadn't left him any choice. She should have realized it was dangerous to try to blackmail someone into being your boyfriend.

He'd made sure she hadn't told anyone about him—his records and his past—before he did what needed to be done. She hadn't.

She didn't have much of a chance, though, to realize her big mistake—that she shouldn't have messed with him. One shove and she was on her way down. And by the time she hit those rocks, she'd probably blacked out.

Grady hopped up on the bed and curled into a ball beside him. Good old Grady. Quinn stretched out one hand and rubbed Grady's ears.

"I really hurt Julie today," he told the cat, "so what can I do to make it up to her, old buddy?"

No reply from Grady.

"I know what I *do* owe her, although she'll never know I was the one who did it."

Those two bums. The muggers from Tara's driveway. It was high time he did something about them. Something permanent. They were probably starting to get over the aches and pains he'd given them. They were probably planning revenge.

He should have taken care of them before, but he'd had too many other things on his mind. Well, better late than never. He'd do it as soon as possible.

He rolled over on his side and immediately fell into a dreamless and untroubled sleep.

CHAPTER SIXTEEN

"Hey, Julie!" Mollie said the next morning, climbing into the car and snapping her seat belt. "I've got something interesting to tell you. I was dying to tell you last night, but you were too busy drooling over that gorgeous hunkerino."

"I was *not* drooling, Mollie. Salivating a little, maybe, but not drooling."

Julie released the hand brake and backed out of the driveway. Her mother was letting her take one of the family cars anytime she wanted now. *One of the benefits of my new maturity*, she thought with a smile. *There's nothing like a big romance to throw you into a whole new league.*

"It's about Tara," Mollie said.

"Tara? She barely even speaks to me these days."

"Then this should dull the pain," Mollie said. "Tommy and I just uncovered the juiciest dirt on sweet little Tara's fancy ancestors."

"How? You don't usually listen to gossip, Mollie."

"No, but this is high-tech snooping, sister dear. It's that new program I got for my computer, the one that allows me to access newspaper files. I found a couple of really neat stories in some old 1920's issues of one of the Richmond papers that said—"

"You can actually do that? Tap into old newspaper files?"

"Yeah. It's great," Mollie said with a grin. "Anyway, it seems that back in the twenties, Tara's family owned Maywood, which was a broken-down wreck, and not much else. They'd lost just about everything in the Civil War and—"

"You mean they were poor?"

"Poor as church mice. Stop interrupting or we'll be at school before I get to all the good stuff."

"Sorry."

"Well, evidently Tara's great-grandaddy decided to do something about the family finances, so he became—get this, Julie—a bootlegger."

111

"You're kidding me," Julie said. "You're talking about Tara's honored and genteel ancestors?"

"That's right. Prohibition was in full swing, so the Braxtons became big-time bootleggers, just like the gangsters in all those movies."

"The newspapers said all that?"

"Well," Mollie went on, "the paper ran this big story because the government was trying to get the goods on them, but the witnesses kept backing out or changing their stories. The Braxtons were poor, but they sure must have known people in the right places. So they eventually got filthy rich via illegal booze. Old Great-Granddaddy Braxton really knew how to recoup his losses."

"The Braxtons, bootleggers," Julie said wonderingly. "Can you imagine? No wonder they could afford all the remodeling and restoration they did on Maywood, not to mention the heated pool and billiard room, *and* that party-sized hot tub Tara goes skinny-dipping in. Well, I'm glad I don't have any secret crimes I'm trying to hide, with the two of you snooping around.

Tara was definitely up to something.

Julie could tell by the way she, Shelley, and

Jessica abruptly stopped talking when Julie came up, unexpectedly, behind them in the hall.

It wasn't the first time something like this had happened lately. The three of them always seemed to have their heads together, plotting.

It was pretty clear to everyone in the school now that Julie was no longer a part of what used to be a close-knit foursome. The three of them had excluded her from all their activities. Not that she minded; she was too busy these days with Quinn to take much notice. It was amazing how he filled her life.

Sometimes, though, she missed their big shopping trips to the mall. That always used to be fun, trying things on and giggling. Tara was a shopoholic and practically lived at the mall. She knew every department of every store and had a sixth sense about when things would be going on sale.

My wardrobe will never be that good again, Julie thought with a sigh. *We did have some good times together.*

But now the other three were up to something.

Well, it can't be too bad, Julie reassured herself. *If Tara thinks she can break up Quinn and me, she's wrong. And that's all that matters now—Quinn, and what we have going for us.*

She went over to her locker and took out the books she would need for first period.

"Something wrong, gorgeous?" said a voice behind her.

"Oh, Brad," Julie said, turning. "You scared me. I was a million miles away."

"So I noticed," he said. "I wish it was me you were with, a million miles away."

He didn't appear to be joking. Brad had changed recently, Julie thought. He'd grown more serious.

"Is that a line or what?" she said lightly.

"It's an 'or what.' It definitely isn't a line," Brad told her.

"If I didn't know you better, I'd think you were for real." Julie tried to cover her growing uneasiness with a laugh.

"It is for real," he said.

People had begun to drift off down the halls to their classes. Julie and Brad were alone in front of her locker. He didn't seem to want to leave her.

She really didn't feel like getting into a big discussion right now with Brad. And where was Quinn? He usually met her before first period.

"Don't you know how I feel about you, Julie?" Brad persisted.

"No. No, I don't," she replied, fiddling with her books, her eyes lowered. This was getting downright embarrassing. "You're such a kidder, Brad. I never know how to take you."

"Take me any way you want, I'm yours! There I go again, acting smart-mouthed. But I do mean it, Julie."

"Since when?"

"Since always. Well, since the big swim party last summer, anyway. You looked so cute in that polka-dot bikini, with the matching freckles popping out across your nose. I thought to myself, 'Hey, what's happening here?'"

"But you never said anything to me until now," Julie said. "Why? If you really felt that way, why didn't you say something instead of acting like a clown?"

Brad shrugged. "Because I was . . . *am* . . . a dumb jerk, that's why. I thought I'd impress you with my wit and charm, but I guess you were looking for a Greek god, not a clown."

"You mean Quinn."

"Yeah, Quinn, God's gift to Braxton Falls. And speaking of Quinn, Julie . . ." Brad's voice trailed off, and he looked uncomfortable.

"What about him?"

"I don't know, exactly. It's just a feeling I have. He's too . . . something. Intense. Brooding. I don't know. I wish you weren't so crazy about him."

Julie opened her mouth to protest, but Brad held his hand up to silence her. "You're a real sensible girl, Julie, but Quinn could be the original Jack the Ripper and you probably wouldn't even notice."

"What a terrible thing to say!" Julie snapped. "Has it ever crossed your mind, Brad, that maybe you're just a little bit jealous of him?"

"Sure I'm jealous of him," Brad said. "Who wouldn't be? He's got you, hasn't he? But that's not why I'm telling you this. If I thought he was right for you, I wouldn't say a word. But I swear, Julie, there's something wrong with that guy. I can feel it in my bones."

"There's absolutely nothing wrong with Quinn! And if that's all you wanted to tell me, I've got to get to class now."

"Okay, okay, if that's how you feel," Brad said. "Uh-oh, here comes your Greek god right now. Talk about jealous. Look at that face! He doesn't want you to be around anyone but him, haven't you noticed? That's not healthy, Julie."

Quinn was walking quickly down the hall toward them. *He must have overslept,* Julie thought. *That's why he's late.* But Brad was right about the expression on Quinn's face. He didn't like her talking to Brad, that was clear.

"I hope you aren't expecting me to duke it out with that guy over you," Brad said. "I don't have a chance against all those muscles. Besides, I faint at the sight of blood. My blood, anyway."

The bell for first period rang.

"Ah, saved—literally—by the bell! I'm out of here," Brad called over his shoulder as he trotted down the hall.

Brad was wrong, Julie thought defensively. Quinn was perfect, just perfect. Maybe he was a little jealous, but he was getting over that. Hadn't they talked all that out yesterday, and hadn't he apologized? It's just that he cared so much for her that he wanted her all to himself now, until they got to know each other better.

So why, then, did she tell him Brad was only getting a history assignment from her? Why was it important to convince him that her conversation with Brad was strictly business? Why did she feel she needed to tell a lie like that?

And why had the look on Quinn's face frightened her so?

Chapter Seventeen

✦

BRAXTON FALLS—The bodies of two young men were found late yesterday afternoon in the woods south of town. They were the victims of apparent foul play.

The bodies, lying in the backseat of a 1989 gray Ford Escort, were discovered by a family hiking in that area.

Each of the victims, who appeared to be in their early twenties, had been dealt a blow to the head. Police found a crowbar next to the bodies. It is estimated the deaths occurred sometime between 10 P.M. and midnight on Saturday.

Traces of drugs and drug paraphernalia have been found in the car, leading police investigators to suspect that the murders were drug related.

Although neither victim carried identification, the car was registered to a Norman Clayborn of Custisville, Virginia. Clayborn was subsequently identified as one of the victims. The other has been identified as Frank E. Soames, also of Custisville. . . .

Norman and Frank.

Norm and Frankie! A gray Ford Escort!

Julie suddenly felt dizzy and nauseated. Those were the two men in Tara's driveway. The ones who'd threatened her. The ones that Quinn had beaten up. It had to be them!

"Are you finished with the front page, Julie?" asked her mother. "There's absolutely nothing in the feature pages this morning. Julie? Are you feeling all right? You look so pale."

"No . . . no, Mom. I'm fine. It's just that I didn't get to bed until late last night."

"I told you so," scolded her mother. "You were out with Quinn until all hours Friday night. And then again last night. Thank goodness the boy had to work Saturday night, or I'd hate to think how exhausted you'd be this morning!"

Julie wasn't listening to her mother.

Those men. Murdered!

Julie could hardly wait to be alone with Quinn at school, in a spot where they couldn't be overheard.

She waited in the school parking lot for him and ran over to his car as he opened the door and unfolded his long legs. She couldn't help admiring Quinn as he smiled at her. But this was not the time for thoughts like that. Hadn't he seen the article in this morning's paper? How could he be so cheerful when *this* had happened?

"Quinn, did you see this morning's paper?"

He nodded. "About those two guys?"

"Yes. Oh, Quinn—they were murdered. With a crowbar! It's so awful!"

Quinn put his arms around Julie and pulled her to him. She could feel his heart beating fast, the way it always did when he held her close.

"I'd say they got what they deserved, Julie," he said gently.

"To be murdered? Nobody deserves that."

"They did. They were going to hurt you." Quinn's voice was grim. Unforgiving.

"Maybe we should have reported what happened to the police," Julie said. "Can we be in any trouble? I mean, can they connect us with those two in any way? What if they find out about what happened in Tara's driveway and think *we* had something to do with their deaths?"

Quinn put his cheek on her hair and rocked her back and forth, the way a mother would soothe an overexcited child.

"Listen to what you're saying, honey," he told her. "You're not making any sense. Why should they think we had something to do with the murders? No one knows anything about what those two tried to do to us. No one except you and me, and neither of us is going to tell the police about *that*, are we?"

"Maybe we should, Quinn."

Quinn stopped rocking and pressed Julie closer to him, resting his cheek on her hair. "Why? Why get involved in something like that? We'd only be asking for trouble, Julie."

"But if—"

"Look, you don't want to go down to the police station and answer all sorts of questions about your relationship with Norm and Frankie, do you?"

"Of course not," Julie said.

"Then leave it alone. You had nothing to do

with their deaths. Besides, think about all the publicity you and your family would get if you—we—got mixed up in this thing."

Julie pictured her mother's reaction and shuddered. "I . . . I guess I just panicked. You're right, of course, Quinn. I haven't told a soul about what happened, not even my sister."

"Good." He released her, putting his hands on her shoulders and stooping down to look into her eyes.

"Those two were bad, Julie. Really bad."

As they walked together toward the school building, Julie could only think how lucky she was to have found someone like Quinn.

Someone strong and dependable.

Someone good.

Someone she could always count on, no matter what.

Quinn's jealousy was growing worse, and Julie didn't know what to do about it. Why was he getting more and more possessive of her every day? Why didn't he want her to talk to or be around anyone but him?

At first Julie thought it was her fault, that she was doing something wrong, or not being understanding enough in some way.

Then at times, in a burst of resentment, she was sure it had nothing to do with her. It was Quinn's fault. His problem, not hers. There was something in him, not her, that made him behave this way. Made him turn sullen and angry whenever any of the guys at school talked to her or paid her compliments, even in fun.

And then she'd remember what he'd told her about his childhood and his alcoholic, abusive father.

"He's the one who broke my nose," Quinn said one night. "I was never anything to him but a punching bag when he had too many. I look a little like my mother, so I guess I reminded him of her. He never forgave her for running off and leaving him, so he took it out on me."

They were alone in Julie's kitchen when he told her this. It was almost midnight and they were having milk and cake, not because they were hungry, but because they always managed to find some way of prolonging their time together.

Julie would never forget the expression on Quinn's face when he flattened the cake with the back of his fork, pressing it into pulp, and said, "And I'll tell you this, Julie. When that guy died, it was the happiest day of my life."

Thinking about his unhappy childhood made Julie love Quinn even more. It made her feel guilty for not being patient enough with him, for not taking into account the fact that, growing up, he'd been starved for love and attention.

And so the cycle would start all over again.

And each new incident made it worse. His jealousy was like a snowball rolling downhill, growing larger and more menacing as it went.

Even a casual conversation outside a classroom now, if Quinn saw it, brought on questions: "What were you talking about with him, Julie?" "Have you two ever dated?" And worst of all, when she *had* dated the boy, "Did you ever kiss him?"

Julie always lied when she answered this last one.

"No, Quinn. He was just a casual date. You know . . ."

"Are you *sure*, Julie?"

Julie would always try to look innocent. But the truthful answer was yes, and she hated having to lie like this all the time. Yes, if she'd dated the guy in question, she probably *had* kissed him.

There had never been anything serious, though, between her and any of those guys. Just a few kisses at parties or at her front door, but nothing hot and heavy.

Julie lied because she wasn't sure what Quinn would do if she *did* admit kissing, however casually, any guy other than him. He would, she knew, consider it a kind of betrayal of him, even though it had happened long before he came into her life.

He hadn't gotten into a fight with any of her old boyfriends over her . . . so far. The word was getting out about him, though, and guys were starting to leave Julie alone.

She resented this. She'd always liked people and enjoyed school, but now she felt as if she had an invisible wall around her.

Well, Quinn would get over this phase. He'd settle in and make friends. It was always hard to start a new school.

Face it, Julie, she thought. *You're making excuses for Quinn and you know it.*

Yes, but what else can I do? The alternative is to break up with him and I could never, never *do that.*

Even Mollie seemed to be looking at Quinn differently now.

"Don't you and Quinn ever double-date or go to parties, Julie?" she asked. "When I see you in the halls or at lunchtime, the two of you are always off together in some corner. Is that right? I mean, is this *really* what you want?"

Mollie must have mentioned this to her mother, because Mrs. Hagan had been coming on strong lately about how the teen years were the time for fun and friendship and lots of school activities.

Even Brad had something to say about it. He took Julie aside one day when Quinn was nowhere in sight.

"Are you and Quinn okay?" he asked. "I mean, does he lock you up in a dark closet if you try to leave your ivory tower or something?"

Julie smiled. "I'm not Rapunzel, Brad. My hair's not long enough."

He didn't smile back. "I mean it, Julie. I know you don't like me to criticize him, but I don't like what Quinn's doing to you. You've still got two years of high school to get through, and he's making a hermit out of you."

Julie sighed. "Don't you start in on me, too, Brad."

"I figured I wasn't the first. Just about everyone has noticed it, Julie."

Julie bristled. "I don't know why everybody's suddenly so concerned about my personal affairs."

"Because there are a lot of people here at Jefferson High who like you. Really like you," Brad said. "Oh, I know you thought Tara and her buddies were your closest friends, but that's a laugh. I'm talking about the kids in your classes. Maybe you don't pal around with them socially, but they admire you and hate to see you get messed up the way you are now."

"Messed up?" Julie shook her head in amazement. "Brad—I've never been as happy in my entire life as I am with Quinn. He's everything I ever wanted in a guy. I'll always feel this way about him."

"Yeah, well." Brad's face fell and his shoulders slumped. Then he gave himself a little shake and said, "I just hope he gets over this jealous stuff, Julie. It's not normal."

"He's not *that* jealous," Julie protested.

Another lie. That was all she seemed to do these days. Nobody had ever told her that love involved a lot of lying.

"Not that jealous?" Brad repeated. "You could've fooled me. One more thing," he said as he turned away from Julie. "Tara's still on your case. Be careful. That girl's a witch with a capital B."

Julie had just about written Tara off as a threat. All the plotting Tara, Jessica, and

Shelley seemed to be doing right after Julie and Quinn paired off had come to nothing.

True, Julie had found a dime-store rubber rat in her locker one morning, but that was all. She figured that's what they had been planning that day they'd been in the huddle. As dirty tricks went, it had been pretty mild.

To her surprise Julie discovered that Brad was right when he'd said a lot of kids at Jefferson High liked her. Now that she'd broken with Tara, Jess, and Shelley, Julie found herself being included in other groups, and receiving invitations to join extracurricular activities that she never would have considered before.

Of course, Quinn objected to anything that would take her away from him.

"What about me, Julie?" he'd ask plaintively. "What am I supposed to be doing when you're running around up to your pretty little ears in rah-rah stuff?"

And then he'd play with her hair or kiss her until she was breathless and she'd forget what it was she'd been saying.

But lately Julie had been giving a lot of thought to what Brad and Mollie had said, and what her mother had implied with her lectures about the necessity for friends and activities in the teen years.

"I've let a lot of activities slide this semester," she told Quinn one night when they'd returned home from a date. "Working on the school newspaper, for example. I haven't pulled my weight on the staff for the past couple of weeks. I think they're about to delete my name from the masthead."

"So let them," he said. "Let somebody else write those stories."

"You don't understand," Julie said, evading his encircling arms. "I like writing, and I'm good at it. It's important to me, Quinn!"

So he'd grudgingly agreed to her working on the school paper.

And that's when things had taken a turn for the worse for her and Quinn.

CHAPTER EIGHTEEN

"This Nick Wells guy, the editor of the paper," Quinn began. Julie knew exactly what was coming next. "Have you ever gone out with him?"

"No," she said firmly, truthfully. "Nick has always had a big thing for Tara, but they only started dating heavily last summer. He's really crazy about her, Quinn."

That seemed to satisfy him for the moment. Then, predictably, he asked, "Are there a lot of guys on the staff of the paper?"

"Only a couple. It's mostly girls. At least during football season."

"What guys?"

"What?"

"What guys are on the staff?"

"Oh, you know, the real grinds."

Julie hated herself for this, for making the serious students sound unappealing, but otherwise Quinn would give her even more flack about working on the paper.

"Are you going to have to work every afternoon?" he asked. "Will it mean you won't have much time for me after school now, Julie?"

"Oh, no, not at all. I'll probably spend only half an hour in the newspaper office a couple of times a week. Most of the articles I'll write in study hall or at home."

It hadn't quite worked out that way, though. By the middle of the second week, Julie found she was working almost every afternoon in the newspaper office with Nick.

She tried to explain the situation to Quinn.

"Nick says he's been getting complaints about how dull the paper is this year, and we're trying to come up with some ideas for new features and columns."

"Just you and Nick?"

"No, there are others, too, usually"—she hoped he wouldn't ask how often she and Nick were alone, working—"but Nick has asked me if I'd consider being feature editor. I'd really like that, Quinn. I think I can do a good job on it."

Quinn reluctantly agreed, but insisted on

waiting for her after school every afternoon and driving her home.

Julie was pleased he wasn't putting up an argument about her new job as feature editor and her long hours. He was taking it well. Maybe they were working out their problems, after all. This jealousy thing of Quinn's would run its course. It had to.

She just wished, though, that Nick didn't always walk her out to the parking lot. She could tell Quinn didn't like that.

"It's just that Nick always thinks of something else he wants to talk to me about, so he follows me out rather than making me stay even later," she explained.

"Yeah, I bet," Quinn said. "If I were him, I'd want to stick around you for as long as I could, too."

One afternoon Nick made the mistake of putting his arm around Julie and giving her a quick hug when they parted.

It was all perfectly innocent. Even Tara and a couple of cheerleaders, who'd just come out of school after rehearsal, glanced over and didn't act as if Julie and Nick were doing anything out of the ordinary.

But Quinn came boiling out of his car, fists

clenched, and strode over to Nick.

"Hey, Nick," he said, "take your hands off my girl."

At first Nick must have thought Quinn was joking, because he laughed. But then Quinn said it again.

"You heard me, take your hands off Julie. Find somebody else to paw."

Nick's face went white, then red. "I wasn't pawing Julie," he snapped. "Why don't you grow up? You're starting to be a real drag with your jealousy bit, McNeal."

Quinn took a step forward, eyes narrowed and lips set in a tight line.

"Quinn, no!" Julie grabbed Quinn's arm and stepped between them. "Don't do this. Please! It was nothing. Nick wasn't doing anything."

Nick put his hands up placatingly. "Look, Quinn, I don't want any trouble with you. It isn't fair to Julie. And besides, I have a thing about not getting my nose broken. If I did something you didn't like, I apologize. So back off, okay?"

"Please, Quinn," Julie pleaded.

Quinn finally nodded, his eyes still narrowed and glaring, and allowed Julie to lead him to his car.

"Listen, Quinn—" Julie began.

"Forget it," he snapped. "I don't want to talk about it."

"I suppose this means you're going to give me a hard time now about working on the paper," Julie said, her voice sharp. "So I'm warning you right now, Quinn—don't. Don't try."

"Is it Nick? Is that why you're being so stubborn about this?" Quinn asked.

His anger had suddenly passed, and now he was looking at her sadly, pleadingly.

His battered-child look, Julie thought, fighting back the impulse to take his face in her hands and kiss him, make him well. *No, he does this to me all the time,* she told herself fiercely. *And, like a fool, I always fall for it.*

"No," she told him. "It isn't Nick. You know it isn't. So why do you do this, Quinn? You've got to stop."

"I'm sorry, Julie. I don't mean to. Something just comes over me and I can't help myself."

Julie knew what he would say next and prepared herself for it. She could almost say it by heart now.

"It's just that I love you so much, honey. . . ."

We can't go on like this, Julie thought. *Talking doesn't seem to help. Maybe if we went to the school counselor, she could help us or tell us where to go to get help*.

But this wasn't the time to bring it up. She'd wait until she and Quinn were alone, and he was feeling mellow. That would be tomorrow night. Friday. They had a big date planned. Dinner in a little restaurant on the edge of town. *That's the right time*, Julie thought. *Tomorrow night . . .*

What a shame he had to act this way today, when she'd thought he was getting better about this jealousy thing. And in front of an audience, too.

Julie remembered the expression on Tara's face as she'd stood watching the exchange between Quinn and Nick.

She'd been smiling.

Quinn stood Julie up for their Friday-night date.

She'd put a lot of thought into what she would wear and finally settled on a dark-gold dress with a flaring skirt and a wide, tight belt. With it she wore the amber earrings and pendant her aunt had brought home from a recent trip to Europe.

The color of the dress brought out the gold

135

flecks in Julie's eyes, and the amber jewelry suited her coloring. This would soften Quinn up and make him agree to a heart-to-heart talk. Something about her coloring turned Quinn on, and she was really playing it up for all it was worth tonight.

At eight-thirty Julie realized Quinn wasn't coming.

All dressed up and no place to go, she thought dismally. *Where is he?*

She tried calling his apartment, but there was no answer.

"Do you suppose something's happened to him?" she asked her parents. "I mean, like an accident or something? Should I call the police?"

"No," her mother said. "Something's probably come up. Maybe they called him in suddenly to work. You said they've done it before. He'll call and explain—just be patient."

But he didn't call. Finally, a little before midnight, Julie went to bed.

She was just falling asleep when she heard a gentle tapping at her window. Her bedroom was on the second floor, overlooking the backyard. At first she thought a branch of the huge old elm tree that grew beside the house was blowing against the window.

But then it came again. Tap, tap, tap. More insistent this time.

She climbed out of bed, shaking back her long hair, and went to the window.

Quinn's face peered in at her. He'd climbed the elm tree and was crouched on a limb outside her window.

"Quinn! What . . . ?" Julie pushed up the window, grabbing her robe from the back of her desk chair and slipping into it.

Quinn crawled through the window. "So you're home." He sounded relieved.

"Sssh!" she cautioned. "You'll wake the family. Of course I'm home. What did you think? And where on earth have you been? I've been worried sick."

Quinn took her in his arms. He was rough, almost hurtful, and Julie was painfully aware that he shouldn't be in her room at this hour, with her parents sleeping just down the hall. What would happen if her mother came in and found her here in Quinn's passionate embrace? She'd ground Julie forever.

"Then you weren't out with Nick Wells?" Quinn asked.

"What? I was supposed to have a date with

you, remember? Why would I go out with Nick Wells, anyway?"

"I've seen the way he looks at you, Julie. And I've seen you looking back at him. You like him, don't you?"

"Oh, no, Quinn! Not *that* again. No, I—"

He overrode her protest. "Why *wouldn't* you have a thing for Nick? He's a real big shot, and his folks are rich and all that."

"Are you out of your mind, Quinn? What's wrong with you? You stood me up and now you come crawling through my window at midnight because you have some crazy idea I've been out with Nick Wells. I don't feel that way about Nick. I never have!"

Quinn's hands tightened on her shoulders. "Do you really mean that, Julie? You aren't just saying that because you're afraid of what I might do to you?"

"*Do to me?* What are you talking about? What made you think I was out with Nick?"

"I saw the note."

"What note?"

"The note from Nick, telling you to meet him at eight at The Point. I went there and waited, but no one came. I thought maybe you two decided to meet someplace else, but I came by the house anyway, just in case. That's when I thought I saw you moving around in your bedroom. So I waited in the car until all the lights went out and—"

Julie was aghast. "You actually thought I'd . . . and you've been watching the house all this time?"

Quinn pulled her more tightly to him, pinioning her arms. She couldn't move.

"Don't try to change the subject, Julie. What about that note?" His voice was quiet and menacing.

"I don't know anything about a note. Are you making this up or what? Let me go. You're hurting me."

Quinn loosened his hold slightly. "I found a note—*the* note—on top of my books this afternoon after school. You'd already left. It was from Nick to you, telling you where to meet him. Nick hates my guts now, after yesterday. I thought he put it there to show me he'd moved in on you."

"It doesn't even make sense," Julie said, shaking her head. "If the note was to *me*, I'd have it, wouldn't I, not him?"

"Yeah, I guess you're right. Maybe Nick was just yanking my chain," Quinn said, after thinking it over for a few moments. "I swear, Julie, I was so freaked out at the thought of him and you, I didn't know what I was doing. I just went crazy, I guess."

Julie struggled to free herself from his grasp. How many times had she heard *that*? How many more times would she hear it?

Quinn pulled her to him again and kissed her hard. As if he were punishing her, showing her who was boss.

There was a light tapping at the door.

"Julie?" Mollie whispered. "Are you all right in there?"

Frantic, Julie pushed Quinn toward the window. "Go. If my parents find out you're here, we're both in big trouble."

When she finally opened the door to Mollie, her sister regarded her suspiciously. "I heard someone talking in here. I didn't know what to think."

"It was the radio," Julie said.

Mollie looked unconvinced, but replied, "As long as you're okay, then. It's just that your voice sounded kind of . . ."

She took another look around the room. "Well, good night, Julie."

Is this a crazy dream? Julie asked herself after

Mollie left. *Did Quinn really crawl through my window and accuse me of secretly dating Nick Wells?*

She put her hand to her mouth. She could still feel Quinn's fierce kiss on her lips.

No, it wasn't a dream.

If only it had been.

CHAPTER NINETEEN

Quinn sat in his car, still staring at the house. He could see Julie's room from this angle. He watched it until the light went out.

His hands were trembling on the wheel. He'd been nearly out of his mind at the thought of Julie—his Julie—out with that stuck-up Nick creep.

He should have known better. Julie wouldn't do something like that. Julie would never betray him.

Betray.

He'd looked that word up in the dictionary once when he and Alison . . .

Well, he'd looked the word up, and it meant "be a traitor to, prove faithless, deliver up to an enemy."

If Julie had gone out with Nick, she'd have been doing all those things. She was his. He loved her and he wanted her to love him the same way. Completely. Totally. And for the rest of her life.

He'd loved Alison that way once. Yes, he could allow himself to think of her now that he was certain he and Julie would be together forever.

He'd fallen in love with Alison—or at least he'd thought it was love—the first time he saw her. Of course, that was four years ago, when he was only fourteen, so what had he known about love then? At the time, though, he'd thought it was the real thing.

How could I have been so dumb? So obsessed? he asked himself. He'd tried to make Alison notice him, even though he knew she was way above him. She was like a princess, and he was just a skinny kid from the crummiest part of town.

Maybe he shouldn't have followed her home from school all the time and hung around her neighborhood day and night, watching her house, but he couldn't help himself.

But Alison didn't like all that attention. Didn't like him trailing her in the halls at school and following her home afterward. She'd complain and tell him off, but her coldness only made him more enchanted, more in love with her.

And then he started watching her through her bedroom window. He found he could hide behind a bush and . . . But that was when her old man caught him and threatened to report him to the police.

He didn't report him, though, not out of kindness but because he didn't want a family scandal. The next day at school Alison had said, "You better leave me alone from now on, Quinn McNeal. Leave me alone or you'll be sorry. Really sorry."

But he couldn't leave her alone. He tried, and it just wouldn't work. He loved her too much.

So that's when Alison and her rich little girl friends and their dumb jock buddies did that terrible thing to him. . . .

Quinn realized he'd been biting his lip so furiously that he'd drawn blood.

I shouldn't let myself think about that night, he told himself. *The shrink at The Place said I have to let it go. It's all in the past now, and there's no reason to hang on to it anymore.*

CHAPTER TWENTY

On Monday morning Julie found Tara, Jessica, and Shelley waiting for her on the front steps of the school, the way they used to before she and Quinn became an item.

There was no sign of Quinn. His car wasn't in the parking lot, either.

I hope he isn't still angry, Julie thought fearfully, rubbing her arms where Quinn had grabbed her Friday night. Something had to be done about Quinn's crazy jealousy. And soon.

Tara came over to her, followed by Shelley and Jessica.

"How was your weekend, Julie?" she asked with a sly smile.

"Fine," Julie said uncertainly, wondering what Tara was up to. It was clear by the expression on Tara's face that it was something nasty.

Julie tried to act normal and casual. "I went—"

Tara interrupted, a look of fake girlish interest on her face. "How was your date with Quinn Friday night? Did you have a good time?"

Shelley and Jessica were exchanging furtive glances. As usual, they were transparently obvious. What were those three trying to pull now?

Julie suddenly realized what it was. *Of course,* she thought. *Why didn't I think of it right away? It was Tara who wrote that note and put it in Quinn's books.*

But why?

To make trouble between us, that's why.

"Why are you interested in my weekends all of a sudden, Tara?" Julie asked.

Tara widened her gray eyes innocently. "Why, Julie, I've always been interested in your love life. Remember when the four of us would tell each other everything?"

"That was then. This is now. And the three of you have been giving me the cold shoulder ever since I started going with Quinn."

Tara sputtered a little protest, but Julie cut her off.

"Obviously *you're* responsible for what

happened Friday night," she said, her anger building.

"You wrote that note, didn't you? And you put it on Quinn's books so he'd be sure to see it. And I know why. You were trying to make trouble between Quinn and me."

She went on, knowing even as she spoke that she was handling the situation badly. She was too angry now. She was losing her head. Her questioning was coming out all wrong, making her seem paranoid and unstable.

"So don't think you're pulling the wool over my eyes, Tara, with your chummy little best-friends act," she concluded. "And if you think you can break up Quinn and me, then guess again."

Tara was regarding her with a look of puzzled concern, one delicate eyebrow raised in ladylike astonishment. Her two hangers-on, Jessica and Shelley, were also playing their parts to perfection, looking at Julie as if she were a raving maniac.

Why are Jess and Shelley doing this? Julie wondered. Were they really *that* much under Tara's thumb? How could they let Tara dominate them the way she did?

Was I that easily led, once?

Not that much, maybe, but yes. Tara led me around by the nose, too. It's good to be free of her now.

"Honestly, Julie," Tara finally said with pretended concern. "I think you're losing it entirely. Why would I try to break up you and Quinn? It was probably just one of those macho male things, you know? We all know Nick and Quinn hate each other's guts after that big jealous act Quinn pulled in the parking lot last week."

The hostile, envious look Tara shot Julie when she said that told her Tara wouldn't mind having Quinn act jealous over *her*.

"So maybe Nick decided to play a little joke on Quinn," Tara went on, regaining her cool. "He knows Quinn would totally hit the roof if he thought you were dating somebody else." Then she said wistfully, sweetly, "I'm just hurt, Julie, terribly hurt, that you would ever think I'd do something like that to you."

I should have known, Julie thought as Tara turned and walked away. *I should have realized that Tara always wins.*

Quinn didn't show up at school until noon. Julie was headed toward the cafeteria when he caught up with her.

She didn't like the way he looked. His lips were set in a tight, thin line, and his eyes were dark and glaring.

He's probably been brooding all weekend about what he thinks Nick did to him, Julie thought with a shiver. *I've got to tell him what really happened before he sees Nick.*

Pulling him aside, she said, "Quinn, listen to me. I know who pulled that trick on us Friday night."

"So do I," he said grimly. "Nick Wells."

"No, it wasn't Nick. It was Tara."

Quinn looked at her in disbelief. "*Tara?* Why would she do something like that? What's she got to do with us?"

His eyes shifted from her face to the far end of the hall. He was still looking for Nick.

"Tara has a lot to do with us, can't you see?" Julie clutched his arm. "She's jealous of me—us—and wants to come between us, so—"

"That's crazy, Julie. You're imagining things. It was Nick, and I'm going to punch him out for it when I see him."

He started to leave, but Julie pulled him back.

"No, Quinn, don't do that! You'll only be making trouble for yourself. You'll be put on suspension for starting a fight. Mr. Reed really comes down hard on things like that."

"I can't help how I feel, Julie. I'd like to smash Nick's face in."

"You don't mean that. I know you, and you couldn't possibly feel that . . . that violent about somebody."

"Then you don't really know me, Julie. There's a lot about me you don't know."

"Promise me, Quinn. You've got to promise you won't hit Nick!"

Julie was trembling. "Please," she repeated. "For me. Please."

"All right," he said, almost as if he were humoring her. "I promise I won't hit Nick."

Was it her imagination, or did he stress the word "hit"?

Quinn's promise, if it really *was* a promise, lasted only until they were seated at a table in one corner of the cafeteria.

Suddenly, glancing across the table, Julie saw Quinn's face change. The dark look of anger came into his eyes. It was a look she was learning to recognize, and dread.

She turned around to see what he was staring at. It was Nick, headed toward his usual table with a loaded tray.

Before she could stop him, Quinn jumped to his feet.

"No, Quinn! You promised," she said, but it came out a whisper.

Quinn walked over to Nick. One corner of Julie's mind appreciatively recorded the fact that Quinn was as lithe and lean as a jungle cat.

And then, just like a cat, he moved. With one quick motion he flipped the tray up and into Nick's face.

Spaghetti and chocolate pudding dripped from Nick's startled face.

"Hey! What the—?" he sputtered. "Dammit, I'm going to get you for this one, McNeal!"

"Food fight!" someone in the cafeteria yelled, but it was quickly squelched.

One of the lunchroom monitors rushed over to investigate. Fortunately it was only Ms. Magnussen, a first-year teacher, so Nick and Quinn were able to pretend that what had happened was an accident and get away with it. Julie hoped Quinn would notice that Nick was no squealer.

As soon as Ms. Magnussen left, Quinn turned on his heel and left the cafeteria. Half sobbing, Julie followed him.

She found him in the parking lot, sitting in his car. She got in beside him.

"We need to talk," she said.

"You've been saying that a lot lately," he replied angrily.

Why did his mouth, that mouth she loved so, twist in a sneer when he said that?

"Yes, I know," she said, trying to sound reasonable and soothing. "But we never have. At least we've never gotten anywhere with it."

"So what do you want to tell me?"

"I don't want to *tell* you anything, Quinn. *Telling* isn't communicating. And we've got to communicate about this awful jealousy of yours."

"Jealousy? Jealousy has nothing to do with what that loser, Nick, did to us."

"That's what we have to talk about," Julie argued. "Nick had nothing to do with it. It was Tara. Tara's trying to break us up."

"What are you saying, Julie?"

"That it was Tara, not Nick, who wrote that note. But what really matters is the way you're acting. Can't you see? You're so jealous and possessive of me. It's gotten worse over the past couple of weeks, and I don't know what to do about it."

"I don't know what you've got to complain about," Quinn said sulkily. "I thought you'd like a guy who acts like he really cares about you."

"I do. Quinn, I love you, but—"

Quinn's sullen look disappeared. He smiled and tried to put his arms around her, but she moved away from him on the car seat.

"No. Please don't do that," she said quietly. "There's been too much of *that*. It only confuses the issue."

"Oh, come on, Julie. . . ."

"Listen to me, Quinn. It isn't good, this jealousy thing. We shouldn't let the fact that we're a couple cut us off from other activities and friendships at school."

Quinn's eyes flashed. "Are you telling me you want to go out with other guys?" he demanded hotly.

His face was wild. Crazy looking. Julie was frightened.

"No, of course not," she said hastily. "Why would I want to go out with someone else? You know how I feel about you. Why, you . . . you're . . . It's just that I think we have a problem we have to work out."

Quinn started the car. He revved the engine, his foot tromping heavily on the pedal.

"I'm out of here," he said curtly. "This conversation's crazy—and getting crazier. I need some space."

Julie got out of the car and went around to the driver's side. She put her head in the window for a good-bye kiss.

"I wish you'd stay and talk," she said.

Quinn didn't reply. He revved the motor again and suddenly the car shot forward. He sped out of the parking lot without a backward glance.

Julie was left standing, shocked. She'd barely had time to withdraw her head and shoulders from the window when he took off.

What if I hadn't? she asked herself, trembling. She pressed her hands to her cheekbones, imagining the crunch of bone if the side of the car had hit her.

I could have been hurt, she thought.

And what was that he shouted at her as he took off? It had been hard to hear him over the squealing of tires as he peeled away.

It sounded like, "Good-bye, Alison!"

The afternoon crept by slowly.

Julie wondered if she should go to the nurse's station and plead sick so she could go home.

She couldn't ever remember feeling this depressed. It almost hurt to draw a breath. She felt
as if there were a tight band around her chest.

But if she did go home, there would be even
more talk around school than there was now.
No, she would make it through the day somehow, and hold her head high, too.

Brad came up to her after English lit and
said, "Look, Julie, I was there in the cafeteria
when Quinn did his fun-with-food thing."

Julie looked at him wearily. "So?"

"So I think you need a friend." He tapped his
shoulder. "You're welcome to cry on this anytime you want, even if it means Quinn will
come and rip my head off."

He spoke flippantly, the way he always did,
but his blue eyes were gentle and concerned.

*And to think I had him pegged for a conceited,
stuck-up playboy,* Julie thought sadly. *I guess he
tried to be a friend all along, but I didn't see it that
way.*

What a shame she wasn't in love with Brad,
instead of Quinn. Wouldn't everything be easy
then?

Brad seemed to read her thoughts. "You
know, Julie, I wish I was able to act real cool and
laid-back around you, the way Quinn does.

Then maybe it would be you and me, instead of you and him. But you're so pretty and sweet and totally lovable, that I get stupid whenever I'm around you. And so I just have to stand up and make a perfect fool of myself."

Julie laughed faintly, near tears. She leaned forward and kissed him lightly on his cheek. "Now, now, Brad. Nobody's perfect."

Brad smiled. But his voice was serious as he said, "Remember, Julie, if you ever want anybody to talk to, I'm here for you. And I'm good at keeping my mouth shut, too, about anything you say."

Julie resisted an urge to cry. Biting her lower lip to keep it from quivering, she said, "Thanks, Brad. You're a good friend. I might take you up on that sometime."

Julie waited all evening for Quinn to call, to apologize, to make things right between them, but the phone was silent.

She couldn't bear to think about how he'd revved his car and sped away like that, nearly ripping her head off.

She would have liked to talk to someone about it, but she was too ashamed. She almost felt as if it were her fault, as if she had done something to deserve the punishment Quinn had just given her.

How can I let some guy take advantage of me this way? she asked herself. Julie wanted no part of this. She didn't want to be anyone's victim.

By the time she reached school the next morning, she was seething with anger. How could she have let Quinn treat her like that?

To make matters worse, she overheard Nick telling everyone that this morning, when he went out to his car, he found his headlights bashed in. Julie didn't say anything, but she had a sickening feeling that Quinn was responsible.

She was at her locker when Quinn came up behind her, lifting her hair and kissing her on the nape of her neck. "Hi, sugar!"

He was behaving as if nothing had happened between them, an innocent smile on his face.

How could he? How dare he think he could treat her the way he had yesterday and then make everything all right with a kiss?

"Leave me alone, Quinn," Julie snapped. "I don't want to talk to you. You owe me an apology for what you did yesterday. And until you do, and until you're ready to sit down with me and talk out our problems, I'd prefer you leave me alone."

She slammed her locker shut, turned on her heel, and left.

Quinn stared after her, but she didn't look back.

CHAPTER TWENTY-ONE

Leave me alone.

Leave me alone, he thought. *Julie. My Julie, and she wants me to leave her alone.*

That was what Alison had said.

Is Julie going to betray me the way Alison did?

No. He refused to believe that. She'd just been a little upset, that was all. But what about? He couldn't remember. His mind was a blank. Yesterday—what happened yesterday—seemed fuzzy. He couldn't remember what he and Julie had done, and why she was angry with him.

He'd have to think about it, figure out what was wrong and what to do about it. No big thing. Julie loved him. Everything would be all right.

He couldn't think straight today, what with this pounding headache. . . .

Again he left school early and went home. Mr. Reed was sure to get him on this one.

Grady greeted him when he entered his apartment. What would he do without Grady?

He lay down on the bed, a cold cloth over his head and Grady nestled close beside him, and slept. His sleep was restless, marred by ugly, troubling dreams. Dreams of broken glass and screams. And blood. Lots of blood.

He awoke trembling and covered with sweat. Grady had wandered off somewhere. When he'd stopped shaking and got his breath under control again, Quinn got up, showered, and dressed. Then he left his apartment and drove over to Poco's Pizza, where he worked.

"Glad you could make it tonight, Quinn," his boss said. "We've got a lot of delivery orders."

One of his last deliveries was for a slumber party. *It must be a birthday*, Quinn thought, *being a weeknight and all*. Most slumber parties were on Friday or Saturday nights. And here it was, nearly midnight on a school night, and those kids were still up and bouncing around.

He pulled up before the house, a large, sprawling ranch style with a vast front picture window. Suddenly he felt almost dizzy with a sense of déjà vu.

He remained in the car, staring through the window at the young girls in the living room, his pizzas growing cold on the seat beside him, the cheese hardening.

They were laughing, he noticed.

Alison and her friends were laughing at their slumber party that night, he thought. *Laughing at me. Laughing because they knew they'd made a real fool of me.*

"Leave me alone," Alison had said. But, of course, he couldn't do that. He'd loved her too much. And he'd been sure that some day soon she'd realize she loved him, too. That was the way with love, wasn't it?

So when he'd received that letter from Alison—and he'd been sure it was her handwriting—he was deliriously happy. Hadn't he known all along that things would turn out this way?

In her letter Alison said she was sorry for the mean things she'd said to him and promised she'd make it all up to him if he'd meet her after dark in the local park, in an isolated spot where the older kids went to make out.

His heart had been beating wildly when he arrived at the park. He could hardly wait to see

Alison. Could hardly wait to tell her how much he loved her.

And then, suddenly, he'd been seized from behind. Alison was nowhere in sight, nor were her silly girlfriends. He was being yanked and dragged around by some big, husky jock types. He knew who they were, even though they wore ski masks. They were three of those older guys Alison and her friends ran around with.

"We're not going to hurt you, kid," one said. "We only want to teach you a little lesson. And you know what that is, don't you?"

He couldn't answer. He was being held too tightly around the neck by a burly arm.

"Well," the voice went on, "since you don't know, I'll have to tell you. The lesson is that in the future, when a girl says to leave her alone, you leave her alone, okay?"

"We're talking about Alison," another said. "She's asked you nicely to bug off, but you won't do it."

Although Quinn put up a fight, he was thrown to the ground. Two of his captors pinned down his arms and shoulders while the third unhooked Quinn's belt and yanked his jeans off.

Then they ran away, carrying his jeans, leaving him there humiliated and half-naked, to make his way home as best he could without being seen.

When he finally reached his house, he was in a terrible state. Alison—his beautiful Alison—had been in on the terrible thing that had just happened to him. She'd written that letter. She'd schemed with that bunch to make a fool of him, and they were probably all together now, laughing at him.

He dressed quickly and got into his father's pickup truck. His father wasn't home. Probably out somewhere with his drinking buddies.

Quinn was too young to drive. Too young for a license, but he knew how to change gears, what pedals to push. He started the motor, and the truck lurched down the street.

He drove toward Alison's house.

All the lights in the house were burning brightly. He drove past slowly, looking in.

It was a sprawling, ranch-style house, with a huge picture window in the living room that looked out over a long, level lawn.

He could see right into the living room. Alison and three of her girlfriends were moving about the room. They were laughing. He was sure they were laughing at him, making fun of him, saying what a fool he was.

Then something came over him. Something he couldn't control.

A red haze swam before his eyes, and before he realized what he was doing, he'd backed the truck up the length of the street, floored the gas pedal, and came at Alison's house at top speed, driving across the lawn and hitting the picture window with a shattering force.

The truck came to a halt against an inner wall of the living room. He saw two of the girls cowering in the corner, screaming. The third was kneeling on the floor crying, and bleeding from the many wounds inflicted by the flying glass.

And Alison . . .

He looked for the girl he loved. He felt his heart wrench, twist, nearly push its way out of his body when he saw her.

She was lying on the floor, a terrible, blood-less shade of white. A large shard of glass, like a crystal dagger, was embedded in her throat.

The truck door was twisted and jammed, but he managed to wrench it open and make his way through the debris of the living room to Alison's side.

She was dead. Alison was dead. He'd killed her.

His lip was bleeding and his head hurt from the blow he'd received in the crash. He felt dizzy. Everything seemed unreal to him.

He was sobbing uncontrollably when the police arrived. . . .

Quinn found himself crying now as he remembered it, just as he had cried four years before.

But Alison did betray me, he thought. I didn't want to believe it at the time, but she did.

The guys in The Place told me that was always the way it was. Even the best ones could get tripped up by a girl. They said nobody believes it, though. Everybody thinks the one he's in love with is perfect. Can do no wrong.

So what about Julie? Will she be like Alison? No, Julie loves me. She'd not faking it. I know she loves me. And yet lately . . .

No. Julie's the real thing. She's my second chance at happiness. My chance to finally do it right. I hurt her somehow, can't remember how, but I have to make it up to her. Somehow.

He started his car and drove away, his pizza undelivered.

CHAPTER TWENTY-TWO

"I've got to see you, Julie. I'm about to go crazy thinking about you." Quinn's voice was low. Sincere. Repentant.

Julie sat up in bed and propped a pillow behind her back. "Quinn, do you know what time it is?" she whispered into the phone.

"I know, but I couldn't sleep. I wondered if maybe you were lying there thinking about me, too."

She had been, but she didn't want to admit that to him. She didn't want to give him any more power over her than he already had. She was still angry with him.

"So what do you want?" she asked coldly.

"I told you. I need to see you. I need to see you real bad."

"Why?"

Julie's voice was remote, hostile, but it was a growing struggle to keep it that way. The sound of his voice over the phone was giving her the usual fluttery, shivery feelings.

"Because I've got so much to tell you. Things have gone bad between us, but I love you, Julie. And I want everything to be the way it was before."

Julie didn't reply, so Quinn said, "I could come over right now, if you'd let me."

"No, not now," she told him quickly. "What would you do, crawl in my window again?"

"Well, maybe you could come out and we could drive somewhere," he suggested.

Julie pulled the covers over her head, so that she and the telephone were in a little tent, a soundproofed cocoon. She was sure Mollie was asleep, but didn't want to take any chances. What she had to say to Quinn was private. Very private.

"Look, Quinn," she said. "I don't think that's a good idea."

"You looked so beautiful that time I came in your window," Quinn said dreamily. "Your face was scrubbed and shiny, and your hair was hanging down your back. I couldn't keep my hands off you."

"That's why it isn't a good idea for us to see each other right now," Julie said sharply.

She took a deep breath and continued. "You know, Quinn, you and I don't do the usual things kids our age do on a date. We don't hang out with a crowd or go to parties. We're always alone, just you and me."

"I thought you liked it that way," he protested.

"I did. I do." she said. "I mean, I like being alone with you, and that's the problem. There's such a thing as too much aloneness."

"Not for two people like us," Quinn said.

"Especially for two people like us," Julie insisted. "What do we do on a date? We go someplace in your car and then we sit and park. And then you start kissing me and I sort of blank out about things—important things like the fact that we don't really know each other. Why can't we do things with other kids? And why can't we talk about it? Why *can't* we discuss your jealousy, Quinn? It's getting worse. It scares me. You acted like a crazy man yesterday."

"Wait a minute," Quinn said. "Let's talk about this kissing in the car stuff, Julie. You know I'd never do anything you didn't want."

"That's the trouble. I do want it. The kissing. The being close to you."

"So," he said, "then what are we doing wrong?"

Julie sighed. "We aren't doing anything wrong, Quinn. It's just that this physical attraction we have for each other is always the center of every date. And if I sneaked out tonight to be with you, we wouldn't talk. You know we wouldn't."

"So what are you saying we should do?"

"I'm saying let's make a date for tomorrow night. A real, old-fashioned date, none of this out-of-the-way parking stuff. Early dinner, maybe. Sixish. It's a school night, remember, and Mom's started cracking down on my curfew. The Calico Giraffe would be nice. It's quiet and cozy. We can sit in a back booth and talk. Only talk."

"Is that what you really want, Julie?"

"It's what *we* really *need*, Quinn."

When Quinn picked her up Wednesday night, Julie was surprised to see a large, fat old cat in the backseat.

"Is this Grady?" she asked. "The famous Grady? I thought I'd never have the honor of meeting him."

She felt so happy, so lighthearted. Grady, Quinn's beloved cat, was a good omen. She had a feeling in her bones that the old cat would bring them good luck. They'd work things out tonight, she and Quinn, she just knew it. They were special. Their love was special. They would talk out their problems and then live happily ever after.

Quinn looked over the back of his seat at Grady, who was gazing out the window, the very picture of injured dignity.

"I hope you don't mind me bringing Grady, but I hated leaving him at home," Quinn said. "I had to take him to the vet's this afternoon for his shots, and he's kind of mad at me. So I figured he'd feel better if I let him come in the car with us."

Julie liked the tenderhearted way Quinn cared for his cat. She deliberately closed her mind to the way he'd acted on Monday, when he'd driven off so abruptly.

The Calico Giraffe was on the same street as the popular local hamburger hangout, and Quinn, who obviously had never been to either before, seemed surprised, then upset at their proximity.

"What's going on, Julie?" he asked suspiciously. "How come you always have to have your buddies close by for backup?"

"Please don't do this," she pleaded. "Don't start in on your jealousy routine again." She reached over and took his hand. "This is the sort of thing we have to talk about, Quinn."

Where was my head when I picked this restaurant for our date? Julie asked herself. *I ought to know that the least little thing sets him off these days. I should have found a place in another part of town. Tara and some of the gang might be hanging out around here, and Quinn is bound to make a scene.*

She'd even overheard Tara and a couple of the others making plans to grab some fast food and then go over to Tara's house. How could she have forgotten? Mr. and Mrs. Braxton were out of town for a few days, so Tara had the place to herself.

Julie knew what that meant—a little party in Tara's famous hot tub. She'd been invited to those parties often enough and had always refused. She was afraid Tara was going to suggest skinny-dipping, and the thought filled her with horror.

As Quinn pulled into a parking spot right across the street from the Calico Giraffe, Julie looked around anxiously for any familiar cars. Much to her relief, she saw none.

Quinn turned off the ignition. "Watch out for Grady," he warned as she opened the door on her side of the car. "He likes to run off to do his thing, and then he gets lost, dumb cat."

Too late. Before Julie could draw the door closed, Grady had slipped past her, his warm, soft fur grazing her ankles, and was now bounding down the middle of the street.

"Grady! Get back here!" Quinn called.

"Grady!" Julie echoed. Then, as she saw an all-too-familiar dark-green sportscar approaching, she called more urgently this time, "Grady!"

But Grady didn't stop.

The green car was traveling fast, and the driver evidently didn't see the cat loping toward it down the center of the street.

"Grady!" Quinn screamed.

There was a thump and a screech of brakes.

Then silence. A terrible silence.

Grady lay at the edge of the street where he'd been flung by the force of the impact. He wasn't moving. A thin line of blood trickled from his nose.

Julie and Quinn ran over to the cat. Quinn dropped to his knees beside it.

"He's dead," Quinn said, picking up the cat in his arms and cradling it, rocking it.

Then, his voice cold and menacing, he said, "They killed Grady."

He said it again, as if he couldn't believe it. "They killed Grady. Murdered him."

Julie knew who "they" were. Tara, for one. It was her little green sportscar that hit Grady, and she'd been behind the wheel.

In a dim recess of her mind, she watched Tara, Nick, Shelley, and Colin get out of the car and come toward them. They seemed to be walking in slow motion, every step taking an eternity.

Finally the four of them reached Quinn and Julie.

"It wasn't my fault," Tara burst out. "I didn't see that cat until it was too late. It just came out of nowhere."

Quinn turned his head and gave her a look of cold loathing. "He didn't come out of nowhere. He was in the middle of the street. You might have seen him in time if you hadn't been speeding. And if you'd had your stupid eyes on the road."

"Now look, Quinn," Colin said, putting his hand on Quinn's shoulder. "I know how you must be feeling right now, but—"

Quinn angrily shook him off. "No, you don't. You don't know how I'm feeling right now. If you did, you wouldn't be standing here. You'd be running like hell."

"Is that some kind of threat?" Tara demanded.

"It's not a threat," Quinn told her. The expression on his face made her take a step backward. "I ought to kill you for what you just did."

"Quinn, please!" Julie cried, pulling on his sleeve.

Quinn ignored her.

"Did you hear me?" he asked Tara. "I'd like to see you dead for this."

"He's gone nuts," Nick said. "Let's get out of here before he does something crazy!"

"But isn't there something we should do?" Shelley protested.

Colin took her arm and pulled her away, toward the car where Tara and Nick were already headed. "Maybe later, when Quinn's got a grip."

They drove off slowly, almost reverently, as if by doing so they could being Grady back from the dead.

A crowd had gathered. The shrieking of the brakes and the drama being played out roadside had attracted a lot of attention. Kids milled around staring, eavesdropping.

"Did you hear what he said?" someone asked. "He wanted to kill that girl."

Julie ignored them.

"It wasn't Tara's fault, Quinn," she said, her lips close to his ear. "It was an accident. Grady was in the middle of the street. Tara didn't see him."

It was like talking to a deaf man.

Finally, gently, she raised Quinn from the ground, her hand on his elbow.

He still clutched Grady to him, his shirt stained with patches of blood.

Julie led him to his car and put him in the backseat with Grady.

The keys were still in the ignition. "You'll have to tell me how to get to your place, Quinn," she said.

Absently, he directed her. She had to ask him at every corner, "Do I keep going, or is this where I turn?"

They finally reached his house. It was a large old Victorian, with gingerbread trim. Quinn indicated, with a nod of his head, his entrance at the side.

Julie opened the door with a key she located

on the ring with the car keys. She stepped back, letting Quinn enter first.

He snapped on a wall switch with his elbow. Then he walked across the room and laid Grady on the sofa.

The apartment, Julie noted, was small and dark, but she was surprised to see how comfortably and tastefully Quinn had arranged it. And it was tidy. Books—there were a lot of them—were lined up according to size in the floor-to-ceiling bookcase, the sofa pillows were plumped up in each corner of the sofa, and the table was waxed and shining.

Julie drifted around the room, not knowing what to do. Quinn was sitting on the sofa beside Grady, lost in a world of his own.

Julie's eyes fell on a color photo propped on the coffee table. At first she thought it was a picture of herself—the resemblance was that strong. But on closer inspection she realized it was someone else.

It was a school picture of a young girl, a girl of about fourteen, and she was smiling into the camera.

Her coloring was the same as Julie's. She had the same long golden-brown hair, and the delicately featured oval of her face closely resembled Julie's.

But what was most amazing were her eyes. They were large and slightly tilted and amber-brown, just like Julie's.

Julie felt as if she were looking at a picture of herself taken two years ago.

She turned to Quinn for an explanation of this mysterious look-alike. But the minute she saw his face, the question died on her lips.

Quinn had picked up Grady in his arms again and had moved to an armchair, one that rocked and swiveled, and was rocking Grady, crooning over him, the way a mother does over a sick baby. There was a wild light in his eyes.

"Quinn," Julie said softly. "We have to bury Grady. You can't keep him . . . like this."

There were spots of blood on the sofa. It was amazing, Julie thought, how such a little bit of blood coming from Grady's mouth had dripped so much on Quinn's shirt and the sofa.

"We could bury him in your backyard, maybe," Julie went on. "Under a bush. That would be nice, wouldn't it, Quinn?"

There was no reply. Quinn sat, rocking, his face distant and brooding.

Julie stayed with Quinn for another hour. Or maybe it was two hours. She had no way of judging time in this shadow world of grief. Quinn didn't look at her once.

Finally, realizing there was nothing she could do, no way of making contact with Quinn, she decided to leave.

Maybe he'll feel better if I leave him alone, she thought.

She called a taxi. When it arrived, she went over to Quinn and said, "I'm leaving now, but I'll come back first thing tomorrow. Call me if you need me."

Quinn gave no sign that he'd heard her.

CHAPTER TWENTY-THREE

Her hands were trembling when she paid the taxi driver.

"Have a nice evening," he said.

As she climbed the front steps, Julie realized that her legs were trembling, too.

She was frightened. Terrified. Something was wrong, terribly wrong with Quinn, and there was nothing she could do about it.

Julie couldn't stop thinking about that look on Quinn's face when he'd turned to Tara and said, "I ought to kill you for what you just did." She felt the hairs on her arms stand on end just remembering it. She wondered if she should call somebody—a doctor, maybe. But what would she say? That her friend was acting extremely grief-stricken because his cat had just been run over? No doctor would be willing to pay a house call for something like that. She let herself into the house and walked slowly up the stairs.

"Julie? Are you okay?"

Mollie stood on the landing, looking curiously at her sister.

"How come you're home so early?" she asked. "I thought you had a date with Quinn."

"Oh, Mollie," Julie began, then burst into tears. "It was awful. Just awful!"

The story came spilling out: the date that was supposed to be their chance to work out their problems. Then Tara running the cat down. And how Quinn had acted.

"And now," Julie concluded, blowing her nose, "he's just sitting there like a zombie, holding Grady."

They were in the kitchen now, sharing a pot of instant cocoa that Mollie had hastily prepared. Ever since they were little, this had been their standard cure for injury and heartbreak.

"He didn't want to talk to you?" Mollie asked.

"No. He acted like I wasn't even there."

"Then I don't know what more you can do, Julie. Maybe he just needs some time alone."

"What really worries me though, Mollie, is

the way he looked at Tara. He was so mad at her. I was afraid he was going to hit her or something."

Mollie was silent. Finally she said, "I heard about what Quinn did to Nick in the cafeteria Monday—the whole school did. I was afraid to ask you about it."

Julie raised her head and looked at Mollie. "Ask me *what* about it?"

Mollie shifted uneasily in her chair. "Well, I guess I wanted to know if he's that hot-tempered all the time."

"Oh, no. No," Julie said hastily. "He and Nick just have this feud going, that's all."

"Is that what you two were fighting about last weekend?"

Julie was stunned. "What do you know about that?"

"A lot more than you think, Julie. I know Quinn was in your room Friday night, for starters. And I know you were arguing about something. I could tell you didn't want anyone to know he was here, so I didn't say anything about it."

Julie took a deep breath and then let it out slowly. "You don't miss a thing, Mollie."

"No, and I've been worrying about you and

Quinn," Mollie said. "I mean, you don't know very much about him, do you?"

"Yes, of course I do," Julie said. "Maybe not *everything* . . ."

"I mean, about his family, and where he was before he came to Braxton Falls. Has he told you anything about that?"

"Well, he did tell me about his father's death, and that his father abused him when he was a child," Julie said. "His mother left him and his father when Quinn was just a baby. It was all so awful, Mollie. I hated to make him think about it. And where he lived before didn't seem that important to me. I figured he'd tell me about it someday."

"Do you know when his father died?" Mollie asked abruptly.

"Yeah. It was only a few days after Quinn came to Jefferson High. Why?"

"So that would make it when? The middle of September?"

"Yes. I think it was around the thirteenth. Why?"

"Well," Mollie said, "there would have to be an obituary for the father, wouldn't there?"

"I suppose so, but—"

"Obituaries usually tell something about the

person. You know, his past, his family. That sort of thing," Mollie said.

"Do you really think you can find out about Quinn and his family from his father's obituary?" Julie asked. "I don't know, Mollie. I don't want to invade Quinn's privacy."

Mollie leaned across the table, waving her cup.

"Look, Julie, if this guy's going to be my brother-in-law someday—and from the way you carry on about him, he just *might*—then I have a right to snoop a little into his family's past. What if he has a cousin with two heads or something?"

"That wouldn't make a bit of difference to me," Julie said.

"If *Quinn* had two heads, it probably wouldn't make any difference to you."

"Are you going to use that new computer program of yours?" Julie asked. "The one that gives you access to old newspaper files?"

"Sure. Tommy and I use it all the time."

"Quinn's father lived in Middledale, though, Mollie. It's a really small town—I don't think it even *has* a paper."

"That doesn't matter," Mollie explained. "The Richmond papers usually pick up obits and news items and things like that from the smaller towns."

Julie took her cup to the sink and rinsed it out, then set it carefully in the drying rack. "I'm still not sure about this—it seems like spying."

"Since when is reading a man's obituary spying?"

"Well, okay. But count me out—I don't think I want to help you with this."

"Suit yourself," Mollie said. "You'd probably only push the wrong key, anyway."

"Julie! Julie, wake up!"

Mollie was leaning over her, shaking her.

Julie didn't know what time it was. She'd lain down on her bed with a book but kept reading the same page over and over again until she'd fallen asleep.

"What's wrong? And what time is it?"

"It's only nine. You haven't been asleep long. I have to show you something." There was a note of urgency in Mollie's voice that immediately brought Julie out of her daze. She slipped off the bed and followed Mollie to her room.

"I was right about the Richmond papers carrying news items from the smaller towns,"

Mollie told her, seating herself in front of her computer.

"News? I thought you were looking up an obituary."

"I was," Mollie said grimly. "But it led to more."

She shoved a computer printout into Julie's hand. "Here's an article about Mr. McNeal's death."

Julie obediently took the paper and began to read aloud.

"R. J. McNeal of Middledale, Virginia, was found dead yesterday, presumably of a fall down a flight of stairs in his home—"

Julie paused and looked up. "This is nothing new, Mollie. Quinn told me this."

"Keep reading," Mollie commanded.

"In order to rule out the possibility of foul play, McNeal's eighteen-year-old son was called in for questioning by the local police—"

She stopped reading again. "Quinn told me this, too. He said something about his father hitting his head so hard at the bottom of the stairs that the police thought maybe he'd been pushed. They ruled the death an accident, though."

"But there's more," Mollie said. "Things I don't think he's ever told you."

Julie picked up the paper again.

"Neighbors revealed that they were aware of several instances of loud quarreling between the two men, and that the son was known to have a violent temper. One neighbor confided that the son had recently been released from a juvenile correctional facility, where he had spent four years' confinement in connection with the manslaughter death of a young girl named Alison Barry. . . ."

Julie slumped down onto Mollie's bed. Her head was spinning and she was afraid she was going to faint.

Mollie dashed into the bathroom and reappeared with a wet washcloth. Julie laid it against her forehead.

"Thanks, Mollie. I'm okay now. It was just the shock."

"I couldn't believe it, either, Julie. Quinn, guilty of manslaughter!"

"There has to be a mistake," Julie said. "Quinn couldn't possibly do something like that!"

But even as she said this, Julie again had an unwelcome image. *I ought to kill you for what you just did,* Quinn had told Tara. *And the expression on his face when he said it!*

"I can't understand it," Mollie said. "He must have been only fourteen years old when he killed . . . when it happened. Her name was Alison. . . ." Mollie's voice trailed away.

Alison. The girl's name was Alison. What did Quinn call me that day in the parking lot when he gunned the car and roared away? Alison? Was that it? "Good-bye, Alison." Yes, that's what he shouted at me. But I didn't think either of us knew a girl named Alison.

"Is there any way we can find the newspaper article about the death?" Julie asked.

"I already did," Mollie said. "I'm not sure you should see it, though."

Julie silently held out her hand for the printout.

"Quinn's name wasn't used, of course," Mollie said. "He was legally a minor, and they never release the name of any minor who commits a crime."

"I know," Julie said. She smoothed the paper nervously on her knee, working up the courage to look at it.

Alison had been killed by a flying shard of glass, the article said.

"A male classmate," Julie read, "who had been stalking her and pressing unwanted attentions on her, in a fit of rage and jealousy, drove a pickup truck through the large picture window of the girl's home, killing her and seriously wounding her three companions. . . ." Julie's voice trailed off, and she looked at Mollie in horror.

Quinn, a killer? The thought made her feel sick.

Julie tried to imagine him at fourteen, angry and embittered enough to drive a car through the window of someone's house. But he hadn't meant to kill Alison. That was something Julie was sure of. He'd been angry, out of control, but not a cold-blooded killer. And he'd been so young.

He must have loved Alison very much. But to get that angry—mad enough to kill—wasn't normal. She couldn't believe that of Quinn. Julie looked up at her sister, her face deathly pale. Mollie eyed her anxiously.

"What time does the library close tonight?" Julie asked.

"It stays open until eleven. Why?"

"They must have all the back issues of the local papers," Julie answered, getting to her feet. "I want—I *have* to read all the local coverage of the killing. I have to see the pictures. Everything."

"Then I'm going with you," Mollie told her.

*   *   *

188

It didn't take the librarian long to find the issues of the small local papers that Julie had requested. The details were the same in all the issues.

And the pictures of Alison, the dead girl, were all the same—a school photograph of a smiling young girl.

Julie recognized it immediately. It was the one Quinn had on the table in his apartment.

Again she had that sensation of spinning, of faintness.

Mollie was peering over her shoulder.

"My god, Julie, she looks just like you!"

The faintness passed, and suddenly Julie could see everything very clearly. Why Quinn had stared at her so intently that first day. And why he'd fallen in love with her so quickly. Why he'd followed her at school, stalked her, always there, always watching her.

Those long, brooding looks. The way he touched her. All because she reminded him of Alison, the girl he'd killed.

He's not in love with me, Julie realized with a feeling of aching betrayal.

Quinn is in love with the ghost of Alison Barry.

CHAPTER TWENTY-FOUR

He knew now what he had to do.

Gently, he laid Grady on the bed and left his apartment, closing the door softly behind him.

She was evil. Tara was evil.

Why hadn't he seen it before?

She'd been masterminding a conspiracy to hurt Julie and him, the way Alison's girlfriends had four years ago.

Yes, Tara had been plotting secretly with the others, telling those rich guys with their sneaky eyes to come on to Julie, so that they could make a fool of him and set him up for some kind of cruel trick, like those jocks did in the park that time.

And then get him to kill Julie, just as he'd killed Alison!

Julie had tried to warn him about Tara, but he hadn't listened. He'd been too jealous, too stirred up to see that these so-called friends of Julie's were playing the same sort of murderous games as Alison's had.

But Tara overplayed her hand when she deliberately ran down Grady. She'd thought she could scare Quinn McNeal, push him around. But she hadn't succeeded. He didn't scare anymore, and all these hours sitting here, holding Grady in his arms, had given him time to think, and he'd figured everything out.

If only he didn't have this headache. This pounding and pounding in his head, as if somebody were in there, beating on his skull. Maybe that was one of Tara's tricks, too. She was evil. Yes, that must be it. Well, it would stop, then, the minute he did what needed to be done.

He laughed softly as he climbed into his car and started the engine. It would be easy, so easy. He knew where they were, Tara and her bunch, the ones who'd killed Grady and were plotting to destroy Julie and him. He'd heard them at school, planning their intimate little party at Tara's house. He'd even heard Tara say with a suggestive giggle that her parents wouldn't be home.

He drove up Tara's long, winding driveway and parked boldly in front of the house. Why hide? He was doing the right thing, after all, protecting Julie from danger.

The front door was open, so he didn't have to jimmy the lock the way one of the guys at The Place had shown him.

He walked through the vast, palatial rooms, listening for *their* voices. Maybe downstairs. Yeah, down where she had her party that night.

He hated them for what they had done and for what they were planning to do. He could feel his rage building, building, as he went down the stairs.

When he reached the bottom, his hands were trembling with fury.

They will pay for this, he vowed silently. *Pay dearly*.

He could hear laughing. He followed the sound down a hall and into the games room with its antique pool table and overhead Tiffany-style light.

On the far side of the room, French doors opened out upon a partially enclosed deck.

They were out there. He could hear high-pitched giggles and the splashing of water.

They were in the hot tub, all four of them, and their backs were toward him.

He stood in the shadows for a moment, deciding what to do next.

The water in the hot tub was warm and bubbling. Steam rose from it, but it was chilly on the deck itself.

He glanced over and saw a portable electric heater, glowing red. Nearby, a pile of clothing was scattered about.

His lip curled with disgust.

What trash, he thought.

He looked again at the electric heater on its long, coiled cord.

He walked quietly over to the heater, picked it up, and called to the group in the tub, "Hey! Remember me?"

He laughed aloud when he saw them turn, startled. Saw the expression of fear that came over each stupid, gawking face.

It was Nick, though, who was the first to realize what Quinn was about to do.

"No, Quinn! Put that heater down. Please, man!"

Then Tara started to whimper. She tried to get to her feet but slipped and fell back into the water.

"This one's for Julie," he called out, and hurled the heater into the hot tub.

There was a sizzling, popping noise. Then sparks and a blue flame.

The four of them began to scream and throw themselves around in the water.

Dancing, he thought, watching them with a satisfied smile. *They look like they're dancing. Hey, they're good. Really good.*

Finally they fell back, unmoving, into the water.

He jerked the heater cord unplugged, ignoring the shock that ran through his arm. Then he circled the tub, pushing their heads under the water for good measure. *Just to make sure*, he told himself. *Better safe than sorry. Anything worth doing is worth doing well.*

He took one long, last look from the doorway as he left.

It was quiet now on the deck, except for the gurgling of the hot tub. It continued to swirl festive little bubbles over the dead limbs of the four bodies bobbing facedown in the moving water.

CHAPTER TWENTY-FIVE

TEEN HOT-TUB SLAYINGS
PRIME SUSPECT STILL AT LARGE
BRAXTON FALLS—The body of their daughter, Tara, and three of her friends, identified as Nick Wells, Colin King, and Shelley Molino, all of this city, were discovered by Mr. and Mrs. Prescott Braxton late Thursday afternoon, upon their return from an out-of-town trip.

The victims, all in their teens, had been electrocuted in the family hot tub.

Although the possibility of accident has not been ruled out, it is, according to local police, highly unlikely.

"A large electric heater was present in the tub and apparently caused the deaths," stated Sheriff James "Dusty" Rhoades, who was first on the scene following a call from the distraught parents. "There is every indication of foul play."

Being sought in connection with the deaths is Quinn McNeal, also of this city and a schoolmate of the victims at Jefferson High School.

According to witnesses, McNeal directed forceful death threats toward the victims, following an incident in which Tara Braxton accidentally ran over and killed McNeal's cat.

"It was terrible, the way he looked at her and said, 'I ought to kill you for what you did,' and, 'I'll see you dead for this,'" stated eyewitness Violet Purdy, who was at the scene at the time. "He had such an awful expression on his face, too, when he said it."

McNeal's fingerprints were found on the Braxtons' front door and on the French doors that lead to the deck and hot tub.

McNeal was recently released from the Juvenile Correctional Facility at Mayfield, Virginia, where he spent four years' confinement in connection with the manslaughter death of a young girl.

McNeal was also questioned recently concerning the death of his father, R. J. McNeal of Middledale, Virginia. He was, however, released when the death was judged to be the result of an accident. The elder McNeal had fallen down the stairs of his home. Death was caused by a head injury and was instantaneous.

Although a massive manhunt has been launched, McNeal cannot be located. His car, a white 1987 Plymouth coupe, is missing. When police searched his apartment, they found the dead body of a large cat lying on the suspect's bed. The cat has been subsequently identified as the one accidentally run over by the car driven by Tara Braxton.

CHAPTER TWENTY-SIX

Ten days had passed since Braxton Falls was rocked by what was now being called "The Hot-Tub Massacre."

It was Halloween. Darkness had fallen. The small children of Braxton Falls, carefully chaperoned by watchful parents, had finished their trick-or-treating during daylight hours and were now home, happily gorging themselves on candy.

It had been a rough ten days.

Julie thought of herself as dead. Her past life, her old friends, the way she'd loved Quinn, were things that should be carved on her tombstone.

The only problem was that, at least technically, she was still alive.

Every morning she'd awaken with a feeling

of despair, knowing she had yet another sad, purposeless day to drag herself through.

On Thursday, the morning after Grady's death, Julie had tried to phone Quinn. She wanted to talk to him before she told her parents what had happened. Before they found out about his past.

There was a question she needed to ask him that couldn't wait. Only one question—the only one that mattered. Had he really loved her? All those times when he'd held her in his arms and told her so, had he meant it, or was he thinking only of Alison?

Julie had felt like a fool as she dialed his number, remembering the way she'd opened herself up to him. The times she'd told him of her intense feelings for him.

She was almost glad when the phone rang and rang and no one answered. She'd looked for him at school, but he wasn't there. And then, that night, she'd heard about the murders. Quinn, a prime suspect, had disappeared.

It was on the six o'clock news. The Braxtons had called the police immediately upon discovery of the bodies.

Julie spent that night and all the next day under sedation. Her mother had called in the family doctor, who'd prescribed something that made her feel sleepy and woozy.

She roused herself from bed only once, to talk to the police, but wasn't able to tell them anything they didn't already know.

Then Julie went back to bed and let Mollie give her a pill that allowed her to float off to a land where everything was pink and beautiful.

The only trouble with pills like that, she soon discovered, is that they make waking up even harder.

She would open her eyes and remember Quinn, and then her heart would start pounding again.

Her mother would appear, fleetingly, at her bedside every now and then, talking about how Julie could have been killed by this maniac. How he'd fooled them all with his perfect manners while, underneath it all, he was a cold-blooded killer!

In a small town like Braxton Falls, any unusual occurrence was a big event. The brutal deaths of four teenagers nearly turned the town upside down.

Grief counseling was available at the high school. Funeral services, attended by hundreds, were held for the four teenagers.

For the first few days people walked in fear, locking doors and not going out at night in case the murderer might be lurking about, ready to kill them, too.

And then the news broke, to everyone's relief, that Quinn had been sighted in southern Virginia, in the mountains just across the border from North Carolina. The net, the police assured everyone, was closing on him. They'd have him soon.

Julie hoped Quinn would escape capture. She knew she'd never see him again, that he wouldn't dare show his face in Braxton Falls for fear of being caught. What he had done was loathsome and unforgivable, but still she hoped he wouldn't be caught.

I can't help it, she thought. *I can't bear the thought of Quinn in prison again. It would be for life this time.* He'd been locked up for four years, and she didn't know how he'd been able to survive even that.

Why, Quinn? she asked herself over and over again. *Why did it have to be this way?*

That Halloween night the neighborhood was quiet, except for the older kids.

Julie was well enough now, the doctor had said, to return to school. She'd been dreading it, dreading the curious stares and whispers. But on Halloween, her first day back, it wasn't like that at all. The other kids were sympathetic and helpful. As Brad said, "You have more friends than you think you do, Julie. At least, they're willing to be your friends if you'll let them."

Because of the deaths, the annual Halloween dance at the high school was canceled, and since many of the students had already had costumes made, groups of them were going from door to door, overgrown trick-or-treaters.

Julie was alone in the house, to her relief. Much as she loved them, she needed a break from her family. Both her parents and Mollie kept telling her she ought to "talk it out," get it out of her system. But Julie wasn't ready for that yet. She hadn't even been able to cry about it. Everyone always said that tears were healing. Well, she wasn't healed yet. Maybe she never would be.

A couple of kids from school, boys, came to the door, and Julie tried to talk and even laugh a little with them. She knew she at least had to *act* normal, even if she didn't feel that way.

Her parents were next door at a party, and Mollie was out with her friend, Tommy. Julie hoped none of them felt they had to rush home just to be with her. They cared about her, and she was grateful for that, but right now she simply wanted to be alone, not with others hovering over her, wanting progress reports on the hoped-for lessening of her grief.

She went to the window and looked out at the dark street, playing with the cord that pulled the drapes.

Across the street someone in a skeleton costume was loitering under a tree. She could see him by the light of the streetlamp. She wondered idly which of her schoolmates he was and who he was waiting for. She hoped he wouldn't come over here. Maybe she should turn off the porch and foyer lights. He might think no one was home and pass her house by.

Before she could, though, the phone rang.

It was Brad. Sweet, thoughtful Brad.

He'd stuck close to her at school, meeting her between classes and taking her off campus to lunch.

"Why are you doing this, Brad?" she'd asked him.

"Don't you know?" he replied.

"Look, I appreciate what you're doing, but I'm not ready for someone else right now," she'd said apologetically. "I might never feel that way about someone again. I'm sorry, Brad, but it's only fair to tell you that, so you won't waste any more time on me."

And then Brad had looked at her, his blue eyes bright and hard. "No time spent with you, Julie, is wasted. You'll get through this someday, and when you do, I'll be ready and waiting. And even if you don't, I'll still be here for you."

That had made her cry, and he'd patted her awkwardly.

Funny how she could cry over little things, like a sudden, unexpected kindness, when she had no tears for the thing that gnawed away at her night and day.

"Do you have a lot of trick-or-treaters?" Brad was asking now.

"We did earlier. Now I'm getting the high-school kids. I guess they want to get some wear out of the costumes they made for the dance."

"Maybe canceling the dance was a bad idea," Brad said. "This whole town needs to get back to normal as soon as possible. But then, it's only been ten days."

Ten days, ten years. Some of us will never get back to normal, Julie thought hopelessly.

"I'd love to come over, if you'd let me," Brad said.

"Thanks, but no. I'm kind of tired. I was just about to go to bed when you called."

There was a slight hesitation on the other end of the line.

"You're sure you're okay?" Brad asked.

"I'm fine. Really. But thanks."

The doorbell rang. Then again, impatiently.

"Uh-oh, the door. Gotta go now, Brad.

"Okay. Sleep tight."

If I only could.

"Who's there?" Julie asked before opening the door.

"Death," said a muffled voice.

What a bore these Halloweeners are, she thought with a resigned sigh.

She opened the door and the figure in the skeleton costume pushed her aside, came into the foyer, and closed the door behind him.

He removed his mask.

Julie gasped and had to put her hand against the wall to support herself. Her knees buckled, and her heart was beating at twice its normal rate.

"Quinn!" she whispered. "But they said you were miles away . . . down by the state border!"

He smiled. The thin white scar that bisected his upper lip gave him the fierce, dashing look of a pirate when he smiled like that. How she'd loved kissing that scar, that pirate's smile . . . once.

"Yeah, I fooled them, the jerks. They must have seen someone who looked like me. No, I've been living out in the woods, waiting for things to cool down so I could come back for you."

"Come . . . come back for me?" Julie echoed faintly.

"Of course. Didn't you think I would?" He tried to pull her to him, but she struggled free.

"No, wait a minute, Quinn. Tara and the rest. Did you . . . are you really the . . ."

Her lips were stiff. She could barely move them. She couldn't say the word "murderer."

"Yes," he said calmly. "I killed them. I had to. I did it for you. For us."

"For *us*? How can you say that? You didn't do it for me, or for us. How could you do something like that? It's so awful. I've been sick for days, thinking about it and hoping—*praying*—that something would happen and we would find out it hadn't been you, after all."

Quinn seemed surprised. "But they had to die. They were evil and they had to die. They were as bad as my father."

"Your father? What's he got to do with it?"

"You mean you haven't guessed? You really didn't know I killed my father?"

Julie pressed her knuckles to her lips to keep them from trembling. Her voice was faint. "No. I didn't know that, Quinn."

"The police were right all along," Quinn said. "I really *did* push him down the stairs. I should have done it years ago. It was so easy. And it left me free to come to you, Alison. To find you again."

Alison?

Julie looked deep into Quinn's eyes. They were glazed, unfocused. Mad looking.

Oh God, Julie thought. *Where are my parents? No! I don't want them to come in right now. He won't hurt me, I'm sure of that, but he might try to do something to them. Maybe he has a knife. Or . . .*

Or a crowbar! Norm and Frankie were killed with a crowbar.

Julie tried to keep her voice level and calm. "And Norm and Frankie. Did you kill them, too, Quinn?"

"Of course, Alison. I wanted to take care of you. They tried to hurt you, so I fixed them. They'll never try to hurt you again. It was my first gift to you—"

He broke off and frowned.

"No. That was my *second* gift to you. Do you remember what my first one was?"

Julie shook her head, her eyes wide with fear.

"Karen Slack," he said proudly.

"Wh-what?"

"I killed Karen Slack. I pushed her off the cliff at The Point."

"Karen?" Julie's voice had become high-pitched, almost a shriek. *Calm*, she told herself. *I have to act calm. Keep everything under control.*

"But Karen didn't do anything to hurt us, Quinn.

His eyes narrowed. "She would have, though. She saw my records. The ones that Mr. Reed kept locked up. And she was going to tell everyone about how I'd been in that prison for juveniles."

He paused and smiled triumphantly. "So I killed her. She deserved it, Alison."

Julie shuddered. Those hands. She almost expected to see blood, the blood of his victims, on them.

He moved toward her and took her in his arms.

She felt a terrible repugnance for him now.

He drew her closer, and she suddenly felt sick

to her stomach. The very scent of him, once so exciting, was making her ill. All the attraction she'd felt toward him in the past had turned to repulsion. Nausea.

Gently, she pulled away from him, swallowing a spasm of nausea as he tried to cling to her.

"So what are you going to do now?" she asked him softly. "The police are looking for you, you know. You can't stay here or they'll find you. You took a real chance coming here to see me."

Quinn laughed. He picked up his mask and put it back on.

Julie could see only his eyes, those wild, mad eyes, glittering behind the mask.

"I have a plan. The perfect plan." He took her arm. "I didn't come here just to *see* you. Like I said, I came here to *get* you. I'm taking you with me. We have to be together, don't we? Always and forever. That's what you want, too, isn't it, my darling Alison?"

CHAPTER TWENTY-SEVEN

Quinn gripped Julie's arm with a heavy hand. There was no way she could wrench it from his grasp, and even if she could, she would never be able to outrun him. She was unable to put up any resistance as Quinn propelled her down the walk to a dark-gray sedan parked a few yards away. It was a very average, inconspicuous-looking car, not likely to draw anyone's attention.

That's why he chose it, she thought.

The street was deserted. Any hope she had of calling for help from passersby vanished.

He helped her into the car.

"This isn't your old one," she said, as if they were on a date. Normal. She had to act normal. "Where did you get it?"

"Let's just say I borrowed it for the occasion,"

Quinn replied, laughing. It was a strange laugh. High-pitched. Giggly.

He was still laughing when they headed out of town. This new mood terrified Julie.

"Where are we going, Quinn?" She tried to sound cool, relaxed.

Quinn wagged a finger before her face.

"It's a surprise," he said. "You'll love it, Alison. It's the perfect way for us to be together forever."

She could see now where they were going. They were on the road to The Point.

The Point. The bluff overlooking the Potomac River and the falls.

The place Quinn had been so afraid Julie had gone on dates.

The place where he'd killed Karen Slack. Julie felt another wave of nausea.

When they reached the turnoff to The Point, Quinn stopped the car, his arms, crossed at the wrist, resting lightly on the wheel.

"Have you guessed my surprise yet, Alison?"

A surprise like Karen Slack got? Julie thought. "No, Quinn, please. Take me home. Oh, please, Quinn!" Julie was sobbing now, too terrified to speak clearly.

Quinn backed up the car, looking over his

shoulder. He seemed to be aligning the vehicle with the observation platform.

A wave of relief swept over Julie. "Where are we going? Back to town?"

"Back? No, Alison, we can never go back. Only forward. The two of us, together forever."

He gazed at her tenderly, lovingly. "Can't you see how perfect it is? Just one moment of flying, and then an eternity of happiness together."

He put the car in overdrive.

Julie knew now what he planned to do. Drive them over the cliff. Kill them both.

"No! No!" she sobbed. "I don't want to die!"

"But we'll be famous, Alison." Quinn sounded surprised and faintly reproving. "Lovers will come up here and be inspired by our love and the beautiful gift we gave each other. Poets will write poems about us. You'd like that, wouldn't you, sweetheart? To have people remember our love forever?"

He reached over and took her hand.

Julie tried to pull her hand from his, but he wouldn't let go.

She went crazy, caught in a frenzy of fear and frustration. Wildly, she yanked on his hand. His grip tightened.

With her other hand she frantically tried to open the car door on her side.

"What are you doing?" he demanded. "Are you trying to get away? Why do you want to spoil things, Alison?"

"Quinn!" Julie cried. "Look at me! I'm not Alison. I'm Julie. Julie! And I don't want to die. I don't want to go over the cliff with you. I don't want to be famous. I just want to live. *Live*, Quinn!" She sobbed uncontrollably. "Please! Please, Quinn!"

He looked at her as if he hadn't recognized her until now.

Through the holes in the death's-head mask, Julie could see his eyes losing their wild look. It was almost as if the old Quinn, the boy she'd loved, was looking out at her again.

"Julie? Julie, is that you?"

"Yes. It's always been me."

"I've been so mixed up. It's like another person comes in and out of my body sometimes."

Quinn released her hand and took off his mask.

His thick, dark hair tumbled over his forehead. For an instant Julie remembered the way he looked the first time she saw him.

"I think I've done some terrible things, Julie."

Julie nodded. "Yes, but we can get help for you. You need help, Quinn."

He smiled a little, that scarred, pirate smile.

Then he ran his hand gently over her hair, caressing every strand lovingly, the way he used to. "I love you, Julie. I'd never hurt you. You know that, don't you?"

He reached across her and opened her door. "Get out of the car."

For a moment she couldn't move. She sat staring at him, her eyes wide.

He leaned over and kissed her gently, his lips warm and smooth. "Get out, Julie."

She crawled out, her legs trembling.

Then Quinn revved the car and floored the gas pedal. The car threw up gravel as it streaked forward toward the observation platform.

Julie had just begun to scream when the car smashed through the railing and went over the cliff.

It seemed to hang in midair for a moment. Then it tipped crazily and fell. She heard a crash and a shuddering echo. She knew the car had fallen among the sharp, jagged rocks that lay, partially submerged, in the river just below the falls.

By the time Julie could make her legs carry her to the edge of the cliff to look down, the car was on fire.

It teetered on the edge of a large, flat rock. The current of the river was making it move back and forth. Soon it would be swept away.

Quinn—was he in that car, burning?

Julie hoped he was already dead. She couldn't bear the thought of him feeling that fire, feeling it consuming his flesh, burning him alive.

But he wasn't in the car. The flames revealed a dark figure, sprawled on a nearby rock. The impact of the crash must have flung him from the car when it hit.

He wasn't moving. He was lying on his back, and his head was twisted at an unnatural angle. His arms and legs were flung out, bent, and Julie saw that they were bent the wrong way.

No one's legs, she thought, with rising hysteria, *bend that way*.

He was dead. She knew, then, that he was dead.

The car tipped back and forth again and then slipped into the river. It was borne, still blazing, downstream.

Julie stood a moment, head bowed, looking down at the broken body on the rocks, feeling a deep, aching pity for Quinn.

She also felt a spasm of loss that would get worse, she knew, before it got better. It would never go away. She knew that. But maybe it would get better.

Julie sat down weakly on the edge of the wooden platform and put her head in her hands.

And then, at last, she cried.

Great, racking sobs nearly wrenched her apart. Tears flowed down her cheeks and she wiped them away with the palms of her hands.

Then she folded her arms on her knees, rested her head on them, and cried some more.

When she was finally done, her eyes were so swollen she could barely see, but she felt better. Cleansed, somehow. At peace.

And then, to her great surprise, she realized she was hungry.

Yes, she was hungry and her stomach was growling. Julie couldn't remember the last time she'd been hungry. Food hadn't mattered to her these past ten days.

And then she thought about Brad. How kind he'd been to her. And she had always thought of him as conceited and silly.

What's the matter with me? she wondered. *What kind of person am I, to be thinking about food and Brad Stafford right now, after what I've been through? After what's happened to Quinn?*

A survivor, that's what.

Maybe there really were such things as survivors. And maybe she was one.

I'll just rest here for a few more minutes, Julie thought. *And then I'll start walking.*

It was a long way back to town.

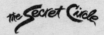